THE TAMING OF THE MAN

A Modern Love Story of Wit,
Chaos, and Culinary Adventures

I0628135

AUREALIA NELSON

AUREALIA NELSON

ISBN 979-8-89778-067-9

Staten House

CONTENTS

DEDICATION

To all the Katherines – past, present, and future – who refuse to be tamed, who embrace their chaos, and who know that true partnership is about mutual respect, not control. This one's for you. May your spreadsheets be ever-organized, your wit ever-sharp, and your relationships ever-satisfyingly complicated. And may you never, ever settle for a man who doesn't know which fork to use. (Seriously, the sheer audacity.)

This book, a cheeky reimagining of a certain antiquated tale of domesticity, is dedicated to the women who have spent centuries battling the narrative imposed upon them. The ones who've subtly (and not so subtly) manipulated the world around them to reflect their own brilliant, messy, magnificent selves. The ones who've re-defined 'taming' to mean something far more empowering than a forced conformity. The ones who have shown the world that a well- placed witticism is often a far more effective weapon than a rolling pin. (Though, let's be honest, a well-aimed rolling pin has its moments.)

It's also for those who've dared to rewrite the rules, to laugh in the face of outdated expectations, and to find joy in the delightful absurdity of love in all its tangled, messy glory.

For the women who've proven that "happily ever after" doesn't mean sacrificing your own identity, your own ambitions, or your own killer sense of humor. It means building a partnership where both individuals can thrive, challenge each other, support each other, and laugh at the ridiculousness of it all.

Because let's face it, relationships are rarely neat and tidy. They're a glorious, chaotic mess of compromises, miscommunications, and the occasional well-timed sarcastic remark. And isn't that precisely what makes them so utterly, hilariously human? This book is a celebration of that mess, of the imperfections, of the hilarious battles of wills, and of the quiet moments of understanding that ultimately bind two individuals together. So raise a glass (of something perfectly chilled, naturally) to the messy, magnificent, utterly untamable women of the world, and to the men who are brave enough to love them.

This dedication is also a tiny, utterly inadequate thank you to all the brilliant women who have shaped my own understanding of love, independence, and the sheer power of a perfectly delivered punchline. To my friends, family, mentors, and fellow rebels who've reminded me, time and again, that we have the strength, the wit, and the unwavering determination to rewrite the narrative – on our own terms.

KATHERINES WORLD

My life is a meticulously curated algorithm. Efficiency is my religion, and my flat in Shoreditch is a testament to my faith. Clean lines, minimalist furniture, a colour palette so restrained it practically whispers, "Order reigns supreme." It's a sanctuary, a haven from the chaotic, unpredictable sprawl of London. Outside, the city thrummed with a million discordant notes – sirens wailing, construction hammering, the relentless drone of traffic. Inside, there's only the quiet hum of my server, a reassuring heartbeat in the digital age.

My friends, bless their chaotic hearts, are the opposite of my carefully constructed world. There's Zara, a sculptor whose studio is permanently draped in a fine layer of clay dust, her hair perpetually escaping its messy bun. Then there's Liam, a musician whose apartment doubles as a rehearsal space, a cacophony of instruments vying for attention. And finally, there's Chloe, a writer whose existence seems to be a constant state of caffeinated inspiration bordering on manic energy. They're all brilliant, wonderfully creative, and utterly bonkers, a testament to my own slightly unconventional taste in companions.

My evenings are usually spent immersed in the world of competitive gaming, my reflexes honed to razor sharpness by years of battling pixelated foes. Or, if I'm feeling particularly cerebral, I'll engage in heated debates about the ethical implications of increasingly sophisticated AI with Liam. These discussions often spill over into philosophical musings on free will versus determinism, a conversation that usually ends with me proving – quite conclusively, I might add – that Liam's understanding of Kant is woefully inadequate. My intellect, you see, is as finely tuned as my apartment.

My days are filled with the satisfying click-clack of my keyboard, as I craft innovative apps designed to streamline the complexities of modern life. I'm not interested in creating frivolous distractions; my apps solve problems, offer efficiency, and generally make people's lives that little bit easier. I find immense satisfaction in optimizing workflows, enhancing productivity, and turning the digital world into a more manageable, predictable space – a sharp contrast to the randomness I experience in the "real" world.

One rainy Tuesday, while dashing between meetings – naturally, all scheduled with military precision – I collided with a man. A monumental collision, actually. Not so much a gentle bump, more of a full-body, slightly undignified tangle. He smelled faintly of old books and something vaguely floral that I couldn't quite place (likely a desperate attempt at masking the underlying aroma of unwashed linen). He had a charmingly disheveled appearance: his hair was a riot of unruly curls, escaping from what looked like a feeble attempt at a comb-over, his clothes were rumpled, and a single sock peeked out from beneath a hole in his trouser leg.

It was, without a doubt, the most disorganized, haphazard, and generally messy encounter of my entire life. And yet, oddly, there was something about him. He apologized profusely, his words tumbling over each other in a flurry of near incoherent apologies that would have sent any sane, organized individual into a state of mild panic. I, however, felt... intrigued. It was like observing a particularly messy piece of abstract art that, despite its chaos, held a strange sort of beauty.

His name, he revealed, was Benedict. Benedict, with his charming smile and utterly chaotic nature. Benedict, who, upon learning that I was an app developer, asked, "Can you make an app to, like, magically clean my flat? Because, let's be honest, my organizational skills are... lacking."

That's when it struck me – a flash of inspiration that was as unexpected as it was electrifying. He was a project. A fascinating, utterly maddening project. A man so utterly devoid of structure, so blissfully unaware of the wonders of a well-organized life, that he practically screamed, "Tame me!"

Now, I'm not one for traditional notions of

"taming." This wasn't about forceful control, about stripping away his individuality. Oh no. My methods would be far more subtle, far more sophisticated. Think of it as a carefully orchestrated symphony of influence, a gentle nudge towards self- improvement. I would guide him, shape him, refine him into a more... acceptable version of himself. Not through brute force, but through the power of strategic manipulation. The power of technology.

And, of course, the power of my superior intellect.

My first tactical move was to subtly introduce him to the wonders of a well-structured to-do list, discreetly sliding a sleek, minimalist digital planner into his hands. His initial reaction was a mixture of bewilderment and mild terror. He looked at the pristine digital interface as if it were a venomous spider ready to strike. I reassured him, deploying my most disarmingly sweet smile, that it wasn't some sort of high-tech interrogation device. It was merely a tool, a pathway to organization nirvana.

The following days saw a series of comically disastrous attempts at following my carefully laid-out schedule. He

arrived late for our second meeting, forgetting his umbrella and looking utterly drenched. He completely missed his bus, spending an hour walking in the rain, which, in itself, was not a problem – the issue arose when he completely misjudged the distance and ended up twenty minutes late for our planned dinner. The dinner, I should add, was at a Michelin-starred restaurant.

This was going to be more challenging than I anticipated. He was resistant to my careful programming, his natural state of chaos seemingly impossible to contain. But perhaps that was precisely what made him so... intriguing. And slightly maddening.

This wouldn't be a quick fix; this was a long-term project, a delightful challenge, a game of strategic wit. And I, Katherine, the master of order and efficiency, was just the woman to win. The initial stages of the taming – let's call it 'refinement' – involved subtle technological interventions. I created a personalized app, cleverly disguised as a quirky game, designed to subtly nudge him toward better hygiene, punctuality, and acceptable social graces.

He didn't suspect a thing, of course. He seemed entirely focused on racking up points and climbing leaderboards, oblivious to the fact that each level he conquered translated into a tiny, almost imperceptible step toward a more refined, organised version of himself. Progress was slow, frustratingly so at times, but I was patient. After all, Rome wasn't built in a day, and neither was a well-organized Benedict. And let's face it, the amusement value alone was almost worth the effort. Almost.

THE ENCOUNTER WITH BENEDICT

The rain, a relentless sheet of grey, mirrored the chaotic state of my usually impeccable hair. It clung to my face, dampening the meticulously applied makeup that usually lasted the entire day, a testament to my commitment to precision. I'd been late for a crucial client meeting – a meeting about optimizing their supply chain, naturally – and now I was even later due to the sudden and violent collision that had sent my perfectly organized tote bag sprawling across the rain-slicked pavement.

The culprit, or rather, the instrument of my sartorial disarray, was standing before me, looking as if he'd just escaped a particularly vigorous tumble in a washing machine. His apologies tumbled out in a breathless rush, a torrent of words that were as disorganized as his attire. He was a study in controlled chaos, his hair a wild storm of curls escaping the confines of what appeared to be a desperate attempt at a comb-over. Water dripped from his coat, creating a small puddle around his feet, and one sock, a rebellious, brightly coloured thing, peeked out from a hole in his trouser leg.

He smelled of old books and something indefinably floral, a desperate attempt to mask what I suspected was the earthy scent of unwashed linen. Everything about him, from the frantic apologies to the damp, mismatched socks, screamed "disorganised." This was a man who was a living embodiment of entropy, a complete antithesis to my carefully ordered world.

And yet, there was something undeniably captivating about the sheer, delightful messiness of him. It was as if he were a

brightly coloured, slightly off-kilter mosaic that somehow, despite its imperfections, held a strange, unsettling beauty.

"I'm so incredibly, terribly, overwhelmingly sorry," he stammered, his words a chaotic jumble. "I... I didn't see you. The rain... the umbrella... it all went rather pear-shaped, didn't it?"

I stared at him, my annoyance slowly giving way to a grudging sort of fascination. He was like a badly written algorithm, full of bugs and unexpected loops, but undeniably intriguing. He was a complete and utter disaster, and yet, there was a certain undeniable charm to his utter lack of control.

"It's quite alright," I said, my voice betraying none of the annoyance churning within. I'd spent years perfecting the art of controlled composure, a skill honed through numerous stressful situations. This, however, was unlike anything I'd ever encountered. This was chaos personified and I, a woman of strict order, was enthralled.

He offered to help me gather my belongings, his movements clumsy but well-meaning. His fingers, stained with something vaguely resembling ink, brushed against mine as he handed me my phone. The contact was fleeting, yet strangely electrifying. It was the most chaotic yet strangely stimulating interaction I'd ever had.

"I'm Benedict," he said, a charming smile lighting up his face despite the rain dripping from his hair.

"Katherine," I replied, my tone even, my expression carefully neutral. I wouldn't let this unexpected encounter derail my carefully planned schedule, not even for a slightly dishevelled man who smelled of old books and desperation.

He then proceeded to confess, amidst another flurry of apologies, that he was late for a meeting at a local library, which involved helping with an exhibition on the history of punctuation - a detail that for some reason only added to his endearing absurdity.

As I surveyed the scene - the scattered contents of my bag, the rain continuing its relentless assault, and Benedict, a charming puddle of apology and disorganisation - a thought struck me. He was a project. A unique, intriguing, and possibly maddening project.

"Are you a developer, by any chance?" I asked, a spark of amusement lighting my eyes.

He looked up, a slight flicker of panic passing across his face. "Yes. I'm, uh, a freelance writer. I... I write about... things."

"I develop apps," I stated, a slight smile playing on my lips. The amusement intensified. "Can you tell me what apps you use daily?" I asked, wanting to understand the extent of his digital footprint.

Benedict hesitated, then shrugged, his eyes widening. "Um, mostly just the weather app, and... sometimes maps. I can't actually remember all of them. I don't really use them that much."

My lips curved into a slight, amused smile. "Interesting," I murmured, my eyes scanning his slightly rumpled clothing, noting the mismatched socks with detached amusement. This man was a walking, talking case study in the art of organised chaos. A project waiting to be undertaken.

Our subsequent meetings were a study in contrasts. My meticulously planned schedule clashed spectacularly with his haphazard approach to time. He was late for every single one, each arrival punctuated by breathless apologies and increasingly elaborate excuses. Once, he arrived with a pigeon perched on his head, an incident he attributed to a series of unfortunate events involving a rogue flock and a particularly aggressive squirrel.

Yet, amidst the chaos and lateness, there was a certain undeniable charm. He was funny, witty, and possessed a self- deprecating humor that was both endearing and disarming.

He challenged my carefully constructed world, introducing a delightful element of unpredictability into my otherwise perfectly ordered life.

And so began my subtle, carefully orchestrated campaign of refinement. It was not about control, but about gentle guidance, about nudging him towards a more... acceptable state of being. It was a game, a strategic challenge, and I, Katherine, was determined to win. My methods were far more subtle than those of a traditional 'tamer'; I used technology as my weapon, subtlety as my shield. I built him apps, carefully designed to improve his punctuality, his hygiene, and even his wardrobe.

The first app, a seemingly innocuous productivity tool, subtly nudged him towards a more organized lifestyle. It started with reminders and to-do lists, progressing to detailed scheduling features that he initially viewed with a mixture of fear and suspicion, but he slowly adapted to this strange yet increasingly effective productivity tool.

His initial resistance was fierce, met with a mixture of charming awkwardness and complete bewilderment. He would arrive for our meetings dishevelled, apologetic, and

generally unprepared, leaving me to wonder if his disorganization was merely a personality quirk or a deep- seated fear of structure.

But as the weeks turned into months, I noticed subtle shifts. His lateness became less frequent, his apologies less frantic, his clothes slightly less rumpled. The pigeons, thankfully, ceased their visits. He even started to embrace the app, using it to schedule appointments and manage his tasks. It was slow, painstaking work, like patiently sculpting a piece of clay, but there was undeniable progress, and progress was a delicious victory in itself.

However, even with my strategic interventions, Benedict remained delightfully unpredictable. He was like a beautifully crafted, chaotic storm; a force of nature that defied categorization, constantly threatening to upset the carefully ordered structure of my life. Yet, amidst the chaos, I found myself increasingly drawn to the fascinating, unpredictable man who had so unexpectedly crashed into my meticulously organized world. It was, I realized, not about controlling him, but about learning to appreciate the beautiful chaos that he brought into my life.

INITIAL
IMPRESSIONS

My initial assessment of Benedict was, to put it mildly, underwhelming. He was a walking, talking embodiment of everything I meticulously avoided in my own life: disorganization, lateness, and a distinct lack of appreciation for the power of a well-structured spreadsheet. He was the antithesis of efficiency, a chaotic symphony of misplaced socks and half-formed apologies. His clothes, perpetually damp and rumpled, suggested a life lived less on a schedule and more on the whims of fate and rogue pigeons. (Yes, there were pigeons involved. Later.) His hair, a perpetually windswept tempest of unruly curls, seemed determined to defy the laws of gravity and possibly common sense.

Even his scent was a testament to his disarray. Old books, yes, I conceded that. A charmingly intellectual aroma, hinting at a hidden depth of knowledge and possibly a slightly dusty library. But underlying the literary fragrance was a distinct undercurrent of... well, let's just say it lacked the crisp, clean sophistication of my usual aromatherapy diffusers. It suggested a life that didn't prioritize daily showers with the same fervor I dedicated to organizing my spice rack alphabetically.

He was, objectively, a mess. A delightful, intriguing, and infuriating mess, but a mess nonetheless. And yet, the very act of categorizing him as "a mess" felt inadequate, somehow diminishing the multifaceted complexity that lay beneath the surface of his organized chaos.

There was something undeniably captivating about his complete lack of control. He was an unpredictable variable in the perfectly balanced equation that was my life, and my

analytical mind, usually so adept at finding patterns and predicting outcomes, found itself utterly baffled by this particular human enigma. This wasn't the polite, predictable social interaction I was used to; this was a genuine, unfiltered, gloriously messy collision.

My initial reaction, however, was purely analytical. This was a project. A fascinating case study in human inefficiency. He was the perfect specimen for my own personal, carefully curated experiment in controlled chaos. I could already imagine the meticulously documented charts and graphs that would result from observing his evolution, or at least, my attempt at shaping it.

But even as my analytical side was already calculating the various data points, another, less rational part of me was stirred. A flicker of amusement, a spark of genuine curiosity, a hint of something that resembled... intrigue. I found myself strangely captivated by his earnest apologies, by the sheer audacity of his lateness, by the fact that a rogue pigeon could somehow become a pivotal point in his narrative.

He wasn't merely disorganised; he was wonderfully, charmingly disorganised. There was a certain inherent honesty in his untidiness, a refreshing lack of pretense that was a stark contrast to the carefully constructed facades so common in my professional world. While others meticulously crafted an image of success, Benedict seemed entirely unconcerned with such trivial matters, happy to let his chaotic energy speak for itself.

His conversational style reflected this inherent disorganisation. His sentences tumbled out in a jumbled mess, a whirlwind of clauses and asides, punctuated by charmingly awkward silences and unexpected bursts of wit. He was a storyteller by nature, weaving tales of misplaced umbrellas and aggressive squirrels with an infectious enthusiasm that, despite my initial skepticism, managed to disarm me.

It was during one of these rambling anecdotes – involving a particularly tenacious squirrel and a stolen croissant – that I realized that my approach to 'refining' Benedict couldn't be merely about imposing order. It had to be something more nuanced, something that acknowledged and respected the quirky, chaotic essence of his being. My initial intention to reshape him into a mirror image of my own controlled efficiency had shifted; now, I saw it as a more delicate dance, a careful negotiation between opposing forces.

I wouldn't force him into a mold; instead, I would attempt to subtly guide him, to help him channel his unique energy into something more constructive. This was no longer a mere project; it was a challenge, an intriguing game of strategy.

And I, Katherine, was determined to play.

My initial assessment had been superficial, overly focused on the external manifestations of his disorganization. But as I spent more time with Benedict, I began to recognize the depth of his character, the sharp intelligence that was hidden beneath the layers of charming chaos. He possessed an innate curiosity, a childlike wonder that was both endearing and inspiring. His passion for the written word, as evident in his slightly ink-stained fingers and his work with the punctuation exhibition, was far more compelling than any wellstructured spreadsheet.

I started to appreciate the sheer artistry of his disarray; the way he seemed to navigate life with a joyful abandon, unconcerned with the constraints of social norms or the expectations of others. This was a man who embraced spontaneity, who saw beauty in imperfection, and who,

despite his frequent lateness and unfortunate encounters with wildlife, seemed remarkably content in his own chaotic skin. The more I observed him, the more I realized that my initial perception, whilst accurate in its description of his outward appearance, failed to capture the true essence of Benedict's character. He was a work in progress, indeed, but one that I found myself increasingly invested in. The project, I realised, was far more compelling than I had initially anticipated. And possibly far more rewarding. The rain, that day, had brought more than just a soggy mess; it had delivered a delightful chaos into my perfectly ordered world, and I, perhaps to my own surprise, was beginning to thoroughly enjoy it.

THE TAMING BEGINS SUBTLY

My first foray into Operation Benedict began, naturally, with data. I compiled a comprehensive spreadsheet – naturally, colour-coded – detailing every observable instance of his sartorial shortcomings, punctuality issues, and questionable hygiene habits. It was a masterpiece of organizational brilliance, a testament to my analytical abilities, and frankly, a little bit terrifying in its scope. Benedict, blissfully unaware of this meticulously documented indictment of his lifestyle, continued his merry dance of delightful disarray. The contrast was exquisite.

The initial phase focused on subtle, almost imperceptible nudges towards improvement. First, the showers. I subtly replaced his rather underwhelming shower gel with a luxurious, cedarwood-infused concoction from a boutique artisan soapmaker. The change was so gradual, so inconspicuous, that even I, the architect of this meticulous plan, nearly missed it. He used it without comment, which, in itself, was a small victory. His usual scent, that peculiar blend of old books and indeterminate dampness, was slowly being overtaken by a more refined, woodsy fragrance. It wasn't an overnight transformation, but a slow, steady evolution that allowed him to adapt without feeling the blunt force of imposed change.

Next came the wardrobe. I started with small, easily overlooked adjustments. A carefully placed, impeccably ironed shirt, casually placed on his chair. A new pair of socks, subtly distinct from his usual mismatched collection. These weren't grand gestures; they were carefully calibrated interventions, designed to spark a quiet revolution in his daily routine. It was a strategy borrowed from classic spy

novels, only instead of overthrowing a regime, I was attempting to subtly nudge Benedict toward a slightly neater existence.

The technology came into play, naturally. I'd already established a sophisticated network of smart home devices, so integrating Benedict into this highly tuned system was relatively straightforward, albeit subtly. His phone, for example, became the epicentre of this subtle technological revolution. I programmed gentle, almost imperceptible reminders for meetings, appointments and, of course, showering. They weren't shrill alarms, rather, soft notifications that appeared at optimal moments, a gentle nudge, as it were. Subtle, sophisticated, and impossible for him to ignore completely. He'd grumble a bit, naturally, but compliance eventually followed. He even started to set his own reminders. A victory for the meticulously planned algorithm and, quite possibly, a win for civilization as a whole.

The kitchen became the site of another gentle but calculated revolution. Benedict's culinary adventures were, to put it kindly, adventurous. I wouldn't say he was a danger in the kitchen, more that his cooking methods displayed a concerning disregard for conventional techniques and health regulations. His attempts at creating a soufflé once led to a small kitchen fire (a testament to his inherent chaotic energy). I began by strategically placing cookbooks on his work table, specifically those focusing on simple, nutritious recipes. The books themselves weren't aggressive; they were subtly positioned, offering themselves as a solution to his less-than-perfect culinary skills. Soon, I noticed a slow but steady improvement in his cooking repertoire. His culinary adventures weren't completely eradicated – a rogue chili pepper still managed to slip into the occasional dish - but they became less... explosive.

The process was far from straightforward. There were setbacks, unexpected deviations from the plan, and the occasional outburst of pure, unadulterated chaos. One morning, I discovered him attempting to make toast using a hairdryer. It was an act of pure, unbridled absurdity, an act of defiance against the carefully constructed order of his life (or, at least, the order I was attempting to impose upon it). I resisted the urge to lecture him and instead, after cleaning the smokefilled kitchen (using my ever-ready smart vacuum, naturally), quietly placed a toaster on his counter.

The hairdryer incident, however, made it onto my data spreadsheet as an unexpected data point, a significant outlier in the trajectory of his development.

My approach was far from dictatorial. It wasn't about imposing my will on him; it was about guiding him, subtly influencing his choices, and gently nudging him towards a more organized existence. It was a delicate dance, a sophisticated game of influence that required patience, precision, and a healthy dose of dry wit. I envisioned our interaction as a complex algorithm, where I would be the programmer subtly changing the parameters, ensuring he moves along the trajectory I desired. He, on the other hand, was the fascinatingly chaotic variable, adding an unexpected charm to the whole experiment.

It became clear, almost instantly, that my initial assessment of Benedict as a 'project' was vastly inadequate. He was far more complex, far more unpredictable, and ultimately, far more fascinating than any spreadsheet could ever reveal. The spreadsheet, while a crucial part of my strategy, remained just a tool. It didn't account for the spontaneous bursts of creativity, the unexpected flashes of insight, or the sheer joyful abandon with which he embraced life's little (and often chaotic) adventures. The data was important, yes, but it

couldn't quite quantify the charm, the humour, the sheer unexpected delight of having Benedict in my life.

While I continued to meticulously document his progress, I also started to appreciate the value of spontaneity, the unexpected beauty in imperfection, the sheer endearing charm of his disorganised charm. I found myself laughing at his clumsy attempts to navigate the complexities of a washing machine, I admired his infectious enthusiasm for badly written novels, and found myself drawn to the unexpected kindness that shone through his sometimes chaotic behavior. The project, I realized, had become something far more meaningful than a mere experiment in controlled improvement. It had blossomed into something unexpected, something genuine, and perhaps, something even... romantic. The 'taming' process, it turned out, wasn't a one-sided affair. He had, in his own delightful chaos, begun to 'tame' me, to reshape my perspective, and open my eyes to the possibilities of letting go of my own carefully constructed systems of order and embrace the beauty of pure, blissful, unpredictable chaos. And, frankly, that was far more exciting than any perfectly organized spreadsheet could ever be.

FIRST LESSONS
IN REFINEMENT

The meticulously crafted schedule, printed on high-quality, recycled paper (naturally), lay before Benedict like a battlefield map. It was a testament to my organizational prowess, a symphony of colour-coded appointments, precisely timed meal breaks, and strategically scheduled "self-improvement" activities. Benedict, however, seemed to view it more as a whimsical suggestion, a loose guideline to be interpreted, rather than strictly adhered to.

His first transgression was, predictably, with the morning routine. The schedule called for a brisk 7 AM wake-up, followed by a precisely timed 15-minute meditation session (guided by a soothing baritone voice, downloaded from a reputable mindfulness app), a 20-minute power yoga session (featuring poses I'd carefully selected for maximum toning and minimal strain), and a precisely timed 10-minute shower using the aforementioned cedarwood-infused soap. Instead, I found him at 8:30 AM, still nestled under the duvet, surrounded by a mountain of discarded novels, his hair resembling a startled crow's nest. The aromatherapy diffuser, placed strategically next to his bedside table, remained untouched, its calming lavender scent lost in the lingering aroma of lukewarm tea and existential dread (one could only assume).

The yoga mat lay forlornly on the floor, a testament to the utter disregard for my precisely-calculated timetable. The meditation app remained dormant on his phone, a silent judgment of his leisurely approach to self-improvement. And the cedarwood-infused soap remained blissfully unused; his usual blend of "old books and indeterminate dampness" still clung to him like a second skin. "Morning, sleepyhead," I chirped, trying to keep the note of barelycontained exasperation out of my voice.

"Mornin'," he mumbled, burying his face deeper into the duvet. His response lacked the enthusiastic gusto one would normally expect from someone who had just completed a rigorous morning yoga session.

"Did you... manage to complete the scheduled morning routine?" I asked, trying my best to maintain an air of nonchalant inquiry, whilst inwardly calculating how much additional time I would need to allocate to compensating for his significant lateness.

"Routine?" he asked, looking around with the

confused air of someone who had just woken from a particularly vivid and nonsensical dream. "Oh, that. Sort of."

"Sort of?" I repeated, my voice dangerously close to a stage whisper. "Sort of how?"

"Well, I did meditate," he said, pointing a finger at the untouched diffuser. "It involved lying here, contemplating the universe."

I resisted the urge to strangle him with my own yoga mat. Instead, I opted for a more refined approach. "And the yoga?"

"Oh, that was too strenuous," he replied with a perfectly innocent expression. "So I substituted it with a light stretch. Sort of." He then winked, adding an unnecessary, and frankly irritating, flourish of charm.

The rest of the day unfolded in a similar vein of meticulously planned chaos. The lunch I had painstakingly prepared – a quinoa salad with grilled halloumi, featuring a delicate balsamic glaze – sat untouched, a silent testament to his unwavering preference for leftover pizza. The afternoon was designated for "cultural enrichment", involving a visit to a highly-rated art gallery, an experience I had anticipated with a mild thrill. Instead, Benedict preferred to spend the afternoon creating, and I use this word extremely loosely, "art" of his own. This involved, in no particular order, smearing paint on canvas in a way that seemed to defy all known principles of artistic expression, and composing a poem dedicated to his "vibrant and chaotic spirit." The poem, however, rhymed "orange" with "door hinge," a feat of unintentional hilarity I could barely contain.

His punctuality, or rather lack thereof, presented a particular challenge. I had scheduled a dinner reservation at a highly-rated restaurant, a place known for its impeccable service and even more impeccable food. Benedict, naturally, arrived forty-five minutes late, sporting a paint-splattered shirt and a look of almost-apologetic mischief. The head waiter, a man known for his stern demeanor and unwavering commitment to punctuality, visibly recoiled.

"My apologies," Benedict murmured, attempting to wipe a stray glob of crimson paint from his cheek. "Got a little... carried away." He then proceeded to regale the waiter with a vivid (and highly embellished) story about his artistic endeavors, completely oblivious to the waiter's rapidly diminishing patience.

Despite the initial chaos and frustration, there was a peculiar charm to his flagrant disregard for my meticulously planned schedule. The meticulously organized spreadsheet, originally intended as a weapon in my campaign of refinement, was

starting to look less like a battle plan and more

like a quaint chronicle of his endearingly disastrous attempts at following instructions.

The evening, however, ended on an unexpected, almost romantic note. After a meal punctuated by Benedict's somewhat inappropriate comments to the sommelier (who, to my surprise, found him strangely endearing), he insisted on walking me home. Underneath a sky scattered with stars, he confessed to finding my obsession with order "charmingly neurotic". And then, he added, without a hint of irony or self-awareness, "I've never met anyone who can colour-code a spreadsheet with such precision."

The compliment, delivered with his usual blend of casual charm and unintentional awkwardness, caught me off guard. It was a strangely tender moment in a day that had been nothing short of a controlled chaos. It occurred to me then, that perhaps, my project wasn't about 'taming' Benedict at all. It was about discovering the unexpected beauty in his chaos, a beauty I could never have predicted from the confines of my meticulously-organized spreadsheet. My 'lessons' in refinement had become, in a rather unexpected turn of events, lessons in appreciating the perfectly imperfect nature of human beings, myself included. The spreadsheet remained, a testament to my original intentions, but its significance was shifting. It was no longer a symbol of control, but a whimsical record of a relationship that was proving to be far more complex, far more entertaining, and far more unexpectedly romantic than anything I had initially anticipated.

DINNER DATE DISASTER

The restaurant, "Le Fleur de Sel," was everything I'd hoped for and more. The ambiance was hushed sophistication, the lighting subtly romantic, and the silverware gleamed with an almost indecent allure. I'd meticulously researched the menu beforehand, selecting a dish that was both delicious and visually appealing – pan-seared scallops with a saffron risotto, a culinary masterpiece designed to impress.

Benedict, however, seemed less impressed and more... bewildered.

He arrived forty-five minutes late, as predicted, sporting a paintsplattered shirt that somehow managed to clash with his already questionable choice of trousers – khaki cargo pants, inexplicably paired with a tweed jacket. The head waiter, a man whose expression rarely deviated from one of polite disapproval, subtly recoiled. I plastered on a smile that felt suspiciously like a grimace.

"Darling, I apologize for the tardiness," I said, my voice laced with a barely concealed edge of icy politeness. "A minor artistic crisis, you see."

Benedict beamed, oblivious to the subtle daggers aimed in his direction. "Indeed! I was wrestling with a particularly stubborn shade of ochre. It had, shall we say, a rebellious streak." He then proceeded to regale the waiter with a dramatic, and entirely fictional, account of his artistic struggle, complete with sound effects and an exaggerated flourish of his paint-stained hands. The waiter, a man who clearly valued his sanity, excused himself with the speed of a startled gazelle.

The meal itself was a masterclass in controlled chaos. I navigated the complexities of the menu with the grace of a seasoned diplomat, ordering wine with an air of confident expertise. Benedict, on the other hand, approached the experience with the enthusiasm of a toddler discovering a mud puddle. He attacked his amuse-bouche with the ferocity of a starving wolf, leaving a trail of crumbs and a faint aroma of indeterminate seasoning in his wake.

"This bread is... remarkably sturdy," he observed, wielding a roll as if it were a small, edible weapon.

When the scallops arrived, a work of art

in themselves, Benedict examined them with the same critical eye he might reserve for a particularly dubious piece of abstract expressionism. "Are these... cooked?" he inquired, poking one tentatively with his fork.

I stifled a sigh. "Yes, Benedict, they are cooked. Pan-seared, to be precise."

He then proceeded to dissect the dish with an almost clinical precision, analyzing its texture, colour, and aroma with the seriousness of a food critic undergoing a mid-life crisis. His pronouncements on the subtle nuances of the saffron risotto were delivered with a gravity that belied their questionable accuracy. "The saffron... has a certain... boldness," he declared, taking a large mouthful that somehow resulted in a tiny risotto-based explosion on his shirt.

The wine list provided a separate source of amusement. Benedict, armed with a seemingly encyclopedic knowledge of obscure hops and malts, approached the sommelier with an air of learned authority. He demanded to know the precise location of the vineyard, the soil composition, and the average rainfall during the grape-growing season, ultimately

confusing the poor man to the point of near-speechlessness. The ensuing discussion on the merits of biodynamic farming lasted a good fifteen minutes, during which I silently assessed the damage to my carefully crafted image of refined sophistication.

I attempted to steer the conversation towards safer topics – the weather, perhaps, or the current state of the global economy. Benedict, however, was not to be deterred. He launched into a discourse on the philosophical implications of eating scallops, a debate that inexplicably veered into a discussion of the inherent flaws in capitalist society and the potential benefits of a return to a preindustrial agrarian lifestyle.

The entire dining experience was, in a word, disastrous. Yet, amid the chaos, I found a strange, unexpected pleasure.

Benedict's blatant disregard for culinary etiquette, his endearingly clumsy attempts at sophistication, and his utterly bizarre pronouncements on everything from scallops to society itself, were somehow... charming. It wasn't the elegant dinner I'd envisioned, but it was undeniably memorable.

It was clear that my carefully constructed plan for refining Benedict was falling spectacularly apart. My attempts at subtle guidance, at subtly shaping his behaviour to fit the norms of polite society, were proving about as effective as using a feather duster to tame a hurricane.

However, it was precisely in this chaos, in this delightful lack of conformity to my perfectly-planned evening, that I began to see something new, something truly unexpected. Benedict's lack of social grace, far from being a source of constant irritation, held within it a captivating rawness, an authenticity that I found surprisingly appealing. He didn't fit

neatly into the pre-conceived mould of my carefully constructed plan, and perhaps, that was precisely the point.

As we walked home under the starlit sky, he confessed that he'd found the entire evening "utterly exhilarating." "It was like a culinary adventure," he enthused, "a gastronomic expedition into the unknown!"

I chuckled, a genuine, unforced laugh. "It was certainly... eventful," I conceded.

"And you," he continued, his eyes twinkling in the moonlight, "you were stunningly composed amidst the utter pandemonium. Like a serene lotus flower amidst a torrent of... risotto."

The compliment, delivered with his usual blend of awkward charm and unintentional silliness, struck me in a rather unexpected way. It was a tender moment, a flicker of genuine connection amid the chaotic backdrop of our disastrous dinner date. And in that moment, under the starry sky, I realized that my carefully planned lessons in etiquette were achieving something quite different than intended. It wasn't about taming him, but about discovering the unexpected beauty in his delightfully unrefined essence.

Perhaps, real refinement wasn't about strict adherence to rules and regulations, but about finding a harmony amidst the chaos. And that, I realised, was a lesson far more valuable than any I could have learned from a stuffy etiquette manual. The spreadsheet, that once stood as a symbol of control, was now starting to resemble a charmingly chaotic map, charting the unexpected course of our evolving relationship. The path ahead remained uncertain, but it felt excitingly so, a wild adventure rather than a predetermined journey. And suddenly, the possibility

of that adventure felt far more alluring than any meticulously planned perfection ever could.

NAVIGATING SOCIAL SITUATIONS

Our next foray into the world of social graces involved a weekend at my aunt's country estate, a place steeped in tradition and, frankly, dust bunnies the size of small rodents. Aunt Mildred, a woman whose spine was as rigid as her corsets (metaphorically speaking, of course, though I wouldn't put it past her), had insisted on a "proper" weekend of country pursuits. This translated into an ambitious schedule involving croquet, afternoon tea, and a rather alarming amount of sherry.

Benedict, bless his paint-splattered heart, approached the experience with the same enthusiasm he'd shown at "Le Fleur de Sel," only this time, his unconventional approach bordered on the catastrophic. He'd arrived wearing a pair of wellies that were clearly several sizes too large, causing him to waddle rather than walk, and a tweed cap perched precariously on his head, perpetually threatening to topple into the perfectly manicured lawns.

The croquet match was a particularly memorable spectacle. Benedict, wielding the mallet like a medieval weapon, managed to knock over not only the wickets but also a rather priceless (and ancient) garden gnome. His attempts at strategic shot placement resulted in a chaotic flurry of mallets, balls, and near misses, leaving a trail of destruction in his wake. Aunt Mildred, her face a mask of controlled fury, could only watch in horrified fascination as her carefully maintained garden transformed into a battlefield. I, meanwhile, found myself struggling to suppress a giggle, the absurdity of the situation proving too much to bear. The sherry, I noted, had a rather helpful effect on the situation.

Afternoon tea proved equally challenging. Benedict, armed with a seemingly bottomless appetite for cucumber sandwiches, devoured them with the gusto of a starving man, crumbs cascading down his shirt and onto his already mud- caked wellies. His attempts at polite conversation involved a rather lengthy discourse on the aerodynamic properties of scones, a topic that seemed to leave Aunt Mildred utterly speechless. I found it rather refreshing to say the least. He then proceeded to enquire about the provenance of the jam, a question which triggered a twenty-minute explanation from Aunt Mildred detailing the history of her family's jam- making tradition, a story that included several mentions of rogue badgers and a suspiciously high number of accidental explosions in the kitchen.

Later that evening, after a dinner that involved a near-miss with a gravy boat and a surprisingly passionate debate on the merits of foraging for wild mushrooms (a debate that ended with Benedict disappearing into the woods with a rather dubious-looking basket), I found myself on the terrace, watching the stars. Benedict, his face smudged with dirt and jam, sat beside me, a contented sigh escaping his lips.

"That was... quite the experience," he murmured, his voice carrying a hint of awe. "I've never seen a badger show so much enthusiasm for jam-making before."

I smiled. "Neither have I," I agreed. And yet, despite the chaos, the neardisasters, and the sheer absurdity of it all, I found myself unexpectedly drawn to him. His clumsiness wasn't simply endearing; it was honest, a stark contrast to the carefully constructed façades of polite society. He wasn't trying to be someone he wasn't; he was simply... him. And that was far more appealing than any carefully cultivated image of refinement.

Our next lesson in social etiquette involved a charity gala, an event that was, by all accounts, a glittering display of wealth, influence, and excruciatingly dull conversation. The atmosphere was thick with the aroma of expensive perfume and the undercurrent of subtle rivalry. I'd anticipated Benedict's presence might cause a few ripples, but I hadn't quite prepared for the tsunami that ensued.

He arrived wearing a brightly coloured Hawaiian shirt, paired inexplicably with a pair of formal trousers, and a look of innocent bewilderment on his face. The shirt itself bore a rather flamboyant tropical motif featuring a rather realistic- looking toucan. He had even somehow managed to get paint on the shirt, somehow, and even a few rogue specks of jam. My carefully constructed plan for a seamless social ascent with him, already rather fragile, shuddered and began to resemble the leaning tower of Pisa. I already knew this evening would be entertaining.

The evening progressed in a manner that could only be described as spectacularly chaotic. Benedict's attempts at polite conversation resulted in a series of rather awkward encounters. He mistook a wealthy philanthropist for a waiter, offering him a rather enthusiastic critique of the canapés. He engaged in a passionate debate on the artistic merits of abstract expressionism with a renowned art critic, causing a near riot amongst the assembled guests. His attempts to charm the host's wife resulted in an impromptu dance-off involving interpretive movements that were both baffling and strangely captivating. Each moment felt like an adventure in itself.

The highlight of the evening, however, involved a rather unfortunate incident involving a rather priceless crystal vase and a rather vigorous attempt to retrieve a rogue strawberry that had escaped onto the dance floor. The result was a

cascading display of shattered crystal and a stunned silence that hung in the air. Even Aunt Mildred seemed to be short of words. Benedict, oblivious to the horror that he had caused, simply beamed. "I caught the strawberry!" he declared triumphantly.

Despite the chaos, despite the shattered vase, and despite the horrified gasps of the assembled guests, the experience felt strangely liberating. Benedict's lack of inhibition, his carefree disregard for social convention, was a breath of fresh air in an atmosphere thick with pretense. His sincerity, his unfiltered enthusiasm, stood out in a sea of meticulously crafted personas.

Later, as we walked hand-in-hand back to the hotel, he confessed that he'd found the entire evening to be "utterly fantastic." "Like a performance art piece," he declared, "a spontaneous explosion of social awkwardness!"

I laughed, a genuine, heartfelt laugh that escaped before I could restrain it. "An apt description," I conceded.

And in that moment, under the quiet glow of the city lights, I realized that my 'lessons in etiquette' weren't about taming him, but about embracing the delightful chaos of his unrefined essence. Perhaps true refinement wasn't about conforming to rigid societal norms, but about finding beauty in the unexpected, and that, I found, was a lesson far more valuable than any etiquette manual could ever teach. The spreadsheet, that once represented a rigid plan, now seemed more like a treasure map, charting an unexpected and exciting journey.

The journey ahead remained uncertain, but the possibility of it, the exhilarating unknown of our unconventional adventure, felt far more appealing than any meticulously

planned route. And in the gentle chaos of our evolving relationship, I discovered a truth far more profound than any rule of etiquette could ever dictate: that sometimes, the most beautiful moments are the ones that defy expectation, and that true connection often flourishes in the spaces between the rules, in the delightful embrace of the wonderfully unexpected.

TECHNOLOGICAL INTERVENTIONS

Our next attempt at social refinement involved a charity gala, a swirling vortex of diamonds, hushed whispers, and an overwhelming sense of impending doom. I had envisioned a strategic deployment of Benedict, a carefully orchestrated dance through the social minefield, but my plans, like a soufflé left unattended, had begun to collapse rather spectacularly. The spreadsheet, once my unwavering guide, now resembled a crumpled napkin after a particularly boisterous dinner party.

Benedict, bless his perpetually mud-splattered soul, had arrived in a rather unfortunate ensemble: a mismatched jacket and trousers, and a cravat that seemed to have been knotted by a particularly enthusiastic octopus. His shirt, a vibrant paisley explosion, was, of course, speckled with paint and, surprisingly, what looked suspiciously like jam. I tried to suppress a sigh. This was going to be... interesting.

The evening began as one might expect, with a series of near-misses and a symphony of awkward silences. Benedict, in a misguided attempt at charm, had engaged in a lengthy discussion on the merits of sustainable agriculture with a renowned taxidermist, resulting in a slightly unsettling

conversation about the nutritional value of badger meat. He'd also mistakenly offered the mayor's wife a canape with his thumbprint firmly embedded in the cream cheese. I noted with amusement that the mayor's wife looked less than pleased.

However, I had a secret weapon in my arsenal: technology. Over the past few weeks, fueled by copious amounts of strong coffee and a healthy dose of amusement, I had

developed a personalized app designed to subtly guide Benedict through the treacherous waters of high society. I'd cleverly disguised it as a bird-watching app, a choice that seemed to perfectly match his rather eclectic interests.

The app, affectionately nicknamed "Project Benedict," was a marvel of modern technology (and my somewhat obsessive tendencies). It contained a discreet timer that gently buzzed whenever it was deemed he'd been engaged in a conversation for too long; a social etiquette cheat sheet featuring handy tips like, "Avoid discussing the merits of badger meat during formal gatherings," and, "Never, ever, offer a canape with a thumbprint in the cream cheese." It even had a silent voice-activated feedback system, which discreetly whispered tips directly into his ear.

The initial results were, shall we say, mixed. The app's attempts to subtly steer the conversation away from the intricacies of Victorian plumbing (a topic Benedict seemed inexplicably drawn to) were met with varying degrees of success. There was the incident with Lord Ashworth, who, after being informed that his prized parrot had an unusual fascination with antique thimbles, abruptly ended the conversation, leaving Benedict looking utterly baffled.

However, the app's time-management feature proved invaluable. It saved us from a disastrous encounter with the notoriously long-winded philanthropist, Mr. Fitzwilliam, who, upon learning of Benedict's keen interest in the migratory patterns of geese, had launched into a detailed and highly technical discourse on the subject that would have taken us well past the midnight dessert. The app's discreet vibration saved the day, though not without several raised eyebrows and muttered comments under the breath.

The real triumph of Project Benedict, however, came at the end of the evening, during the charity auction. The highlight of the event, a priceless diamond necklace, had been put up for bidding. Benedict, in his usual fashion, had initially become captivated by a rather detailed conversation on the ethical sourcing of the diamonds with the auctioneer. I discreetly pressed a button on my own smartphone, which was linked to the app. A soft, almost imperceptible hum alerted him to the fact that his current topic was of less urgent importance than acquiring a very expensive diamond necklace for me.

With a slight cough and a sheepish grin, he'd raised his paddle at the right moment, expertly outbidding the rather formidable Duchess of something-or-other. He'd won the necklace. It was absurd, and utterly perfect. He'd won the necklace, and learned a valuable lesson about strategic timing.

The app also subtly corrected his posture, reminding him to stand up straight and maintain eye contact (which he'd previously been rather neglectful of). It even provided carefully selected conversation starters, ones that were designed to appeal to the particular interests of the individuals he was speaking to, although they sometimes veered off into unexpected territory. One particularly memorable conversation revolved around the surprisingly complex social structures of bee colonies, a topic that inexplicably captured the attention of the rather stern- looking Lady Beatrice. I have yet to understand how bees got into the conversation, but I still chuckled to think about it.

The evening ended, not with a bang, but with a series of carefully orchestrated triumphs. Benedict, slightly dishevelled but undeniably charming, had navigated the

treacherous waters of the charity gala with unexpected grace and skill. He had even managed to charm the notoriously difficult Lady Penelope, a feat I had considered impossible. The secret weapon of "Project Benedict" had, I realized, succeeded in not taming his unique essence but refining it.

The app was a guide, a playful nudge in the right direction, and not a restrictive straitjacket.

As we walked hand-in-hand under the city lights, he confessed that he'd found the entire evening to be "utterly fascinating." "Like a complex game of chess, but with less strategy and more unexpected moves," he added with a grin, "though I'm still trying to figure out why everyone seemed so interested in bees."

"Bees are complex creatures," I responded with a smile, secretly appreciating the unexpected twists and turns of our unorthodox relationship. The app, I realized, wasn't about controlling him; it was about empowering him, giving him the tools to navigate a world he didn't quite understand, to engage in that world with his own unique charm and grace. It was about celebrating, not controlling, his idiosyncrasies.

It was a subtle form of tutoring, using technology to bridge the gap between his natural enthusiasm and the demands of social etiquette, which was much more effective than any dry manual could ever be. The spreadsheet was a thing of the past; we now had something far more dynamic and entertaining, a flexible map that allowed us to adapt and navigate the journey together.

The subsequent weeks brought forth new challenges and new opportunities to test and refine "Project Benedict." We tackled formal dinners, country house weekends, and even a rather intimidating opera performance, each encounter proving to be a unique chapter in our evolving relationship.

The app became less about correcting his behaviour and more about enhancing his already unique charm. It was no longer a means to an end, but a playful partner in our unconventional dance through life. And in the ever-evolving world of modern romance, that, I decided, was the best lesson in etiquette I could ever hope for. The 'taming' wasn't about conforming, but about finding a balance between two different worlds, and using technology to help bridge that gap in a funny, and surprisingly effective way.

UNVEILING BENEDICTS PAST

Our evenings together, punctuated by the beeps and whispers of Project Benedict, gradually transitioned from navigating social functions to deeper conversations. He'd become more relaxed, less prone to impromptu discussions on the migratory patterns of geese, and surprisingly adept at small talk. The app, I realised, was less a tool for control and more a facilitator of connection. It had become the catalyst for a far more intimate understanding of the man beneath the paint-splattered shirts and mismatched trousers.

One cool autumn evening, curled up on his rather surprisingly comfortable sofa – a relic from a bygone era, I'd discovered – surrounded by a chaotic collection of books, paint tubes, and halffinished canvases, he revealed a piece of his past I hadn't expected. It wasn't a dramatic confession, delivered amidst a thunderstorm, but a quiet narrative revealed between sips of Earl Grey tea and the gentle crackling of the fireplace.

He spoke of a childhood spent in a bustling city, overshadowed by a relentless work ethic and the weight of unspoken expectations. His father, a renowned architect, had instilled in him a deep-seated devotion to precision and detail, a devotion that had manifested itself, rather ironically, in a chaotic whirlwind of artistic expression. The meticulously crafted blueprints and the perfectly aligned bricks of his father's creations found their counterpoint in Benedict's own canvases, bursts of vibrant colour and texture that defied any sense of order.

"He wanted me to follow in his footsteps," Benedict confessed, swirling the tea in his cup, his gaze drifting

towards the paintings lining the walls, each a testament to his inherent rebellion against structure. "To be a respectable architect, a pillar of society, all the things I'm decidedly not." He chuckled, a selfdeprecating sound that held a hint of melancholy. "I rebelled in the only way I knew how: chaos."

His rebellion, he explained, wasn't born of spite, but of a need for selfexpression. The precision of his father's world had been suffocating, leaving him yearning for the freedom of vibrant colours, the uninhibited flow of creation, the joy of unbridled spontaneity. His disorganised nature, the paint stains, the perpetually mismatched attire—these were not signs of carelessness, but symbols of his struggle to reconcile his inherent nature with the expectations imposed upon him.

This revelation struck me with surprising force. It humanised him, stripped away the caricature I'd initially perceived and revealed a sensitive soul grappling with a complex relationship with his past. He wasn't simply a man who needed 'taming'; he was a man wrestling with a deep-seated conflict between his inherent creativity and the pressures of a traditional, structured life. My initial amusement at his eccentricities gave way to a deeper understanding and, quite unexpectedly, a surge of empathy.

The conversation drifted to his early artistic endeavors. He spoke of his first exhibitions, his early struggles to find his artistic voice, his moments of doubt and self-criticism. He described the feeling of vulnerability that accompanied the act of sharing his creations with the world, a feeling amplified by the weight of his father's expectations.

He showed me a photograph, a faded image of a young man, his eyes bright with a youthful passion that resonated through the years. He stood proudly beside a vibrant canvas,

its colours seemingly bursting from the frame. The image contrasted sharply with his present-day disheveled appearance, the gap between the man he was and the man he was striving to become, a testament to his ongoing journey of self-discovery.

"I spent years trying to meet his expectations," he confessed, his voice barely above a whisper. "Trying to fit into a mold that wasn't meant for me. I chased precision, order, the things he valued. But I was slowly killing myself in the process."

His story wasn't simply a tale of artistic rebellion; it was a universal narrative of self-acceptance, of breaking free from imposed expectations, of finding one's own path in the face of adversity. He'd spent years striving for a level of order that clashed profoundly with his creative spirit, a spirit that manifested itself in his colourful chaos.

He hadn't simply been disorganized; he'd been actively rejecting a predetermined path, carving his own way through the world, however messy and unpredictable it might be. It wasn't a lack of discipline; it was a conscious, if somewhat unconventional, assertion of his artistic identity.

His past explained not only his messy habits but also his endearing vulnerability. The paint stains on his clothes became symbols of his commitment to his art, the mismatched outfits a testament to his unconventional spirit. Even his obsession with the migratory patterns of geese, once a source of amusement, became a metaphor for his own life's journey, a testament to his inherent search for meaning and beauty in the world around him.

Understanding his past fundamentally shifted my perspective. He wasn't an unruly child requiring taming; he

was an artist fighting to reconcile his innate creativity with the constraints of societal expectations. The 'Project Benedict' app, once a tool to navigate social gatherings, now felt different. It wasn't about correcting him; it was about supporting him, empowering him to navigate a world that often failed to accommodate his unique talents.

As our conversation drew to a close, the firelight dancing across his face, I realized my own preconceived notions had been shattered. The 'taming' I'd envisioned was a far cry from the mutual understanding we'd cultivated. The real transformation wasn't about forcing him to conform to my expectations, but about helping him reconcile his past with his present, accepting him for the wonderfully messy, brilliant artist he truly was. My task, I realised, wasn't to tame him, but to cherish his beautifully chaotic essence.

The following weeks were a departure from the structured regimen of "Project Benedict." The app was still installed on his phone, but its use dwindled as we found a new rhythm, a shared understanding that transcended the rigid protocols of etiquette. We explored art galleries together, discussed his paintings with the kind of insightful conversations I'd previously relegated to theoretical analysis in dusty academic papers. He started to take more pride in his appearance, not because he was striving for some unattainable level of refinement, but because he felt more confident, more comfortable in his own skin.

His artistic flair even began to subtly influence my own life. I found myself incorporating his unpredictable energy into my work, injecting a dose of creative chaos into my meticulously organized routine. The spreadsheets were still there, of course, but they no longer dictated the entirety of my existence. I learned to appreciate the beauty of the unplanned, the unexpected detours that could lead to surprising discoveries.

Our relationship, previously a playful experiment in social engineering, had evolved into something far deeper, far more meaningful. The initial goal of 'taming' had been replaced by a shared journey of selfdiscovery, a testament to the fact that genuine connections transcend the limitations of societal expectations and the constraints of preconceived notions.

The 'taming,' I realised, had been a mutual process, a journey of understanding, acceptance, and the unexpected beauty of embracing the wonderful, glorious chaos of life. And that, I decided, was a far more rewarding lesson than any etiquette manual could ever teach.

A SHIFTING DYNAMIC

The shift wasn't sudden, like a dramatic plot twist in a cheap romance novel. Instead, it was gradual, subtle, like the changing of seasons – almost imperceptible at first, yet undeniable in its eventual impact. One evening, while discussing the merits of various shades of cerulean (a debate that had, admittedly, lasted far longer than it should have), Benedict surprised me. He'd meticulously cleaned his studio, a feat that felt as improbable as a spontaneous eruption of order in a hurricane. The paint tubes were neatly arranged, brushes washed and displayed like a miniature, surprisingly elegant army, canvases stacked with the precision of a seasoned curator.

I stared at the transformed space, my meticulously crafted mental spreadsheets suddenly feeling inadequate, even irrelevant. It wasn't just clean; it was... organized. The chaos had been tamed, not by my app, but by him. And that, I had to admit, was a slightly unnerving development. My carefully constructed game plan, the meticulously designed "Project Benedict," seemed to have taken on a life of its own, evolving beyond my initial intentions.

He caught me staring, a sheepish grin spreading across his face. "I thought... maybe a little tidiness wouldn't hurt," he mumbled, a hint of nervousness in his voice. It was the most conventionally 'acceptable' thing he'd ever done, and yet, it felt strangely rebellious, a silent declaration of independence from the chaotic persona I'd come to know, and perhaps, rather selfishly, come to appreciate.

That evening, we didn't delve into the intricacies of the proper way to hold a champagne flute or the nuances of a

perfectly executed bow. Instead, he showed me a new painting, a breathtaking landscape of rolling hills and vibrant sunsets. It was a departure from his usual abstract style, a deliberate attempt at precision, a subtle nod to his father's legacy, perhaps. There was a newfound balance, a harmony between the controlled and the uncontrolled, reflecting the evolving dynamic in our relationship.

The following weeks were a fascinating study in the unexpected. Benedict began to exhibit a curious awareness of social niceties, not out of forced compliance but a genuine desire to connect. He remembered birthdays, even sending small, thoughtful gifts – a vintage book on bird migration (naturally), a quirky ceramic mug with an equally quirky drawing, a beautifully framed photograph of one of his landscapes. These weren't grand gestures, but small acts of kindness, carefully chosen, revealing a thoughtful consideration I hadn't previously witnessed.

He even started dressing, dare I say it, with a touch more... coordination. His clothes weren't suddenly impeccably tailored, far from it. But the clashing colours seemed less random, the combinations slightly more deliberate. It was as if he'd discovered a new palette, one that allowed for artistic expression even in his attire. It wasn't about conformity; it was about self-expression through a different medium.

The power dynamic, once firmly in my court, began to subtly shift. The app, Project Benedict, became less a tool for control and more of a record of our shared evolution. I found myself consulting it less often, relying instead on instinct and observation. My initial amusement at his eccentricities gave way to a deep appreciation for his unique blend of creativity and unexpected charm.

One rainy afternoon, while watching a particularly poignant documentary on the social lives of penguins (another one of his obsessions), he surprised me again. He reached for my hand, a simple gesture, yet profoundly meaningful. There was a gentleness in his touch, a vulnerability that disarmed my carefully constructed defenses. In that moment, I realised the "taming" process had become something entirely different.

It wasn't about moulding him into an acceptable version of a man, but about embracing the complexities of his personality. The meticulously planned "Project Benedict" had, in a strange way, inadvertently paved the way for a deeper, more genuine connection. My initial plan to refine him had morphed into something more organic, more profound – a shared exploration of each other's unique complexities and unexpected delights.

We started having long conversations about everything and nothing. His artistic process, my research, the absurdity of reality TV, the existential dread of encountering a particularly aggressive squirrel in the park – topics that spanned the chasm between my academic world and his artistic one, a fascinating blend of the intellectual and the whimsical.

His increased self-awareness didn't diminish his creativity; it enhanced it. His artwork became richer, more textured, reflecting a newfound sense of self. He wasn't abandoning his inherent chaos; he was integrating it with a newfound sense of discipline and purpose. He was, in essence, refining himself from within, not from the outside.

And me? I found myself changing too. His infectious enthusiasm for life, his unwavering commitment to his art, his unexpected acts of kindness – they were chipping away

at my own rigid structure, injecting a much-needed dose of spontaneity into my meticulous routine. I started to appreciate the unplanned moments, the detours that led to unexpected discoveries, much like the paths his brushstrokes took on the canvas.

One evening, while sipping wine on his balcony, overlooking the cityscape bathed in the warm hues of sunset, he confessed something unexpected. "You know," he said, his voice soft, "I was terrified at first. I thought you were going to... to change me."

I smiled, a genuine smile, unburdened by the weight of expectation or the pressure of a carefully crafted plan. "I tried," I admitted, "but you surprised me."

The truth was, he hadn't needed taming. He'd only needed understanding, acceptance, and perhaps, a little encouragement to embrace the brilliance that was already within him. My "Project Benedict" had been a detour, a rather circuitous route, but it had ultimately led us to a far more rewarding destination – a genuine connection, forged not through control, but through mutual respect and the discovery of our shared humanity amidst the delightful chaos of life.

And so, the lessons in etiquette were ultimately rendered obsolete, replaced by far more valuable lessons in understanding, compassion, and the surprising beauty of embracing the glorious messiness of human connection. The paint splatters, the mismatched socks, the unpredictable bursts of creativity – they were no longer flaws to be corrected, but rather, the vibrant colours that made Benedict's life, and by extension, my own, a richer, more vibrant masterpiece. The "taming" had been mutual, a shared journey of self-discovery, revealing the truth that true

connection lies not in control, but in the celebration of our shared, beautiful, and utterly chaotic humanity. The final chapter, it seemed, wasn't about taming anyone, but about embracing the untamed spirit within us all. And that, I realised, was a far more compelling narrative than any carefully crafted plan could ever hope to achieve.

KATHERINES
INTERNAL CONFLICT

The rain hammered against the windowpanes, a relentless rhythm mirroring the tempest brewing within me. It wasn't the meticulously planned tempest of "Project Benedict," that carefully orchestrated campaign to refine Benedict into a palatable version of a modern man. This was something... different. Something far less predictable, far less controllable. And honestly, rather terrifying.

My initial amusement, that detached, almost clinical observation of his eccentricities, was dissolving, replaced by a disconcerting warmth, a fuzzy feeling that threatened to unravel the tightly woven tapestry of my carefully constructed life. I'd always prided myself on my rationality, my ability to analyze, dissect, and ultimately, control. And Benedict, with his chaotic charm and unpredictable outbursts of genius, was proving to be a rather formidable opponent in this unexpectedly intimate game of intellectual chess.

I found myself lingering longer in his studio,

drawn not just by the vibrant chaos of his artwork, but by the quiet intensity of his focus, the way his brow furrowed in concentration, the almost imperceptible twitch in his left cheek as he wrestled with a particularly stubborn brushstroke. It was mesmerizing, this raw, untamed energy, and the longer I watched, the more acutely aware I became of my own rigid structure, my own carefully constructed walls beginning to crumble under the relentless assault of his... well, him.

One evening, while he was lost in a world of swirling pigments and abstract forms, I found myself unconsciously reaching for one of his paintbrushes, a thin, delicate instrument that felt strangely comforting in my usually

precise, perfectly manicured hand. I traced the outline of a halfformed shape on the canvas, a fleeting gesture, impulsive and unplanned. It felt... liberating.

The impulse surprised me. I, Katherine, the mistress of precision, the queen of schedules, had acted on impulse. The horror! The sheer, unadulterated audacity of it! Yet, rather than recoil from this unexpected act of rebellion, a strange sense of exhilaration coursed through me. It was a whisper of something new, something unknown, something exhilaratingly dangerous.

My internal monologue, that ever-present

voice of reason and sarcastic commentary, had fallen silent, replaced by a cacophony of conflicting emotions. Amusement warred with intrigue, detachment battled with... what was this?

Affection? The very idea felt alien, a foreign invader in the carefully fortified citadel of my heart.

The carefully crafted spreadsheets of Project Benedict, my digital roadmap to refining the man, began to gather dust. My app, once my primary tool of control, was becoming a relic, a testament to a past ambition that no longer felt relevant. I found myself relying less on strategic planning and more on... intuition. On observation. On something far less predictable, far less scientific. On feeling.

The realization was unsettling. Was I... falling in love? The very notion was absurd. Love was messy, chaotic, unpredictable. It was the antithesis of everything I valued, everything I'd meticulously constructed my life around. Yet, here I was, staring at a half-finished painting, feeling a profound sense of connection to the man who'd created it, a connection that went far beyond the carefully curated parameters of my initial project.

I started noticing things. Small things. The way he hummed off-key while working, the way his eyes crinkled at the corners when he laughed, the way he always left a small, perfectly formed pile of paintbrushes by his easel, a silent declaration of his own inherent order amidst the apparent chaos. These were details I'd previously overlooked, deemed insignificant, yet now they painted a vivid portrait of a man far more complex, far more endearing, than my initial assessments had allowed.

The meticulous detail I applied to my academic work, my research, my strategic planning, was all there, yes, but it was starting to feel... constricting. It felt like wearing a tailored suit in a hurricane – appropriate for the occasion, perhaps, but ultimately, suffocating. Benedict's life, on the other hand, felt like a vibrant watercolour painting, bold strokes of vibrant colour intermingled with delicate washes of softer hues, a testament to the beauty of the unplanned, the unexpected, the glorious messiness of life.

My carefully constructed defenses, those ironclad walls I'd built around my heart, began to crumble under the relentless assault of his infectious enthusiasm, his unwavering commitment to his art, his surprising acts of kindness. It wasn't just his transformation; I was changing too. The rigorous structure of my life, once a source of pride and comfort, now felt like a cage.

His unconventional ways, once a source of amusement, now held a certain... charm. The very things that had initially irritated me – his messy studio, his mismatched socks, his penchant for obscure documentaries about penguin mating rituals – now felt endearing, a testament to his unique spirit, his untamed creativity. He wasn't trying to impress me; he was simply... being himself. And that, I realized, was far

more appealing than any carefully constructed facade could ever hope to be.

The rain outside had finally subsided, the storm replaced by a gentle drizzle, a soft, cleansing rain that mirrored the quiet transformation occurring within me. The meticulously planned "Project Benedict" had been a journey, not to a destination, but through myself. And what I discovered along the way was something quite unexpected – a feeling that was both exhilarating and terrifying, a feeling I could only describe as... love. A love that wasn't about control, but about acceptance, about embracing the beautiful, chaotic messiness of human connection. A love that, much to my own astonishment, had completely and utterly upended my world. And for the first time in a long time, I found myself feeling not fear, but a thrill of anticipation, a sense of exhilaration at the possibility of this new, unexpected adventure. The untamed spirit I had sought to tame in him had, in a surprising twist, awakened something equally wild, equally beautiful within me. And that, I realised, was the most compelling story of all.

BENEDICTS TRANSFORMATION

The initial shock of my own unexpected feelings had begun to settle, leaving behind a quiet hum of... something. It wasn't the sterile, calculated contentment I'd envisioned for myself. This felt warmer, fuzzier, less like a perfectly executed algorithm and more like a Jackson Pollock painting – vibrant, chaotic, and utterly captivating. And Benedict, the subject of my meticulously planned experiment, was at the heart of this beautiful mess.

He, surprisingly, was adapting. Not in the robotic, programmed way I'd initially anticipated, but in a genuine, almost organic evolution. His improvements weren't mere concessions to my demands; they stemmed from a burgeoning self-awareness, a quiet recognition of his own potential. He started taking initiative, small gestures at first – tidying his studio (though "tidy" was still a relative term, a carefully orchestrated chaos replacing the previous free-for- all), actually remembering to put his dirty socks in the hamper (a monumental achievement, I'd admit), and even, gasp, attempting to coordinate his clothes. It wasn't perfect, of course. He still occasionally sported mismatched socks – a charming quirk I now found oddly endearing, rather than a glaring flaw – but the effort was undeniable.

His culinary skills, once a disaster zone, started showing promising signs of improvement. He'd moved beyond reheated instant noodles, embracing simple, fresh ingredients. His attempts at cooking were still occasionally disastrous, resulting in culinary calamities that left me choking back laughter, but the sheer effort, the earnest attempt to please (me, of all people), was unexpectedly touching. I even caught him once attempting – and failing

spectacularly – to bake a cake. The result was a lopsided, slightly burnt creation that tasted alarmingly like charcoal, but it was presented with such earnest pride, such childlike innocence, that I couldn't bring myself to criticize. I ate a sizable portion anyway, mostly to avoid hurting his feelings. It was, perhaps, the most moving act of culinary terrorism I'd ever witnessed.

His artistic endeavors blossomed. His abstract expressionism continued, a testament to his untamed spirit, but a newfound precision was beginning to emerge. His brushstrokes, once wild and chaotic, now demonstrated a greater control, a finer sensitivity. He began experimenting with different mediums, exploring new techniques, pushing the boundaries of his creativity. His latest series, inspired by our own peculiar relationship, I suspected, was a breathtaking exploration of contrasts – sharp lines juxtaposed with soft curves, bold colours contrasted with delicate washes, chaos balanced by a surprising sense of order. He was, quite unexpectedly, becoming a better artist. And a better man.

This transformation wasn't merely about changing his habits; it was a deepening of his self-awareness, an awakening of his potential. He began reading, not just obscure documentaries about penguin mating rituals, but classic literature, philosophy, and even, horror of horrors, self-help books. He'd discovered a thirst for knowledge, a genuine desire to improve himself, not just to appease me. The man who once dismissed my suggestions with a wave of his hand now eagerly sought my opinion, his questions thoughtful, his engagement sincere. He was actually listening, really listening, and not just waiting for his turn to speak.

One evening, while discussing the nuances of Hemingway's prose, he looked at me, his eyes reflecting the flickering candlelight, a sincerity in his gaze that took my breath away.

It wasn't the calculated look of a man trying to charm me; it was the genuine, vulnerable expression of a man discovering himself, a man finding his voice, a man who was, quite astonishingly, falling in love.

I, of course, was in no position to be surprised by that particular revelation. My own feelings, initially a source of bewilderment and fear, were now a swirling maelstrom of emotions – exhilaration, uncertainty, a tremulous hope. My meticulous planning, my carefully constructed strategies, all seemed utterly irrelevant now. The spreadsheets gathered dust, the app remained unused. The perfectly curated life I'd spent years crafting was now crumbling beautifully, like an ancient castle surrendering to the inexorable tide of time.

The change in Benedict wasn't just external; it was internal. He was less reckless, less impulsive, yet equally vibrant, equally captivating. The underlying chaos remained, a vibrant energy that I now found myself drawn to, rather than repelled by. It was like watching a raging fire transform into a comforting hearth, the untamed flames now contained within a structure that enhanced, rather than extinguished, its inherent beauty.

We began spending our evenings in a different way. The intellectual sparring, the playful disagreements, remained, but they were now infused with a deeper connection, a shared understanding that transcended the simple game of wit and sarcasm. We talked, really talked, about our dreams, our fears, our vulnerabilities. It was terrifying, liberating, and utterly exhilarating all at once. I found myself opening up to him, revealing aspects of myself I'd carefully concealed for years. The iron walls I'd built around my heart, those carefully constructed defenses against vulnerability, were crumbling, brick by brick, replaced by something far more fragile, yet far more beautiful.

He started painting me, not as a detached observer, but as a subject worthy of his attention, his admiration. He captured the complexity of my emotions, the subtle nuances of my personality, not in the way of a superficial portrayal, but in a manner that struck a deep chord. He saw me, truly saw me, beyond the carefully constructed persona, beyond the impeccable façade.

Our relationship, once a calculated experiment, had transformed into something far more profound, far more meaningful. It was a testament to the capacity for change, not just in one person, but in both of us. Benedict's transformation wasn't just about conforming to my desires; it was about discovering his own strength, his own potential, his own identity. And in that journey, I discovered my own. I had set out to tame him, but in the process, he had, quite inadvertently, set me free. The unexpected feelings I'd initially resisted were now a tidal wave, carrying me towards a future I could never have imagined, a future that was both exhilarating and terrifying, a future filled with love, laughter, and the glorious, beautiful messiness of a life lived fully and authentically. The rain had stopped. The sun was shining.

And for the first time in a long time, I felt truly, utterly, and completely alive.

A TRIP TO THE COUNTRYSIDE

The countryside air, thick with the scent of wildflowers and damp earth, was a stark contrast to the sterile modernity of our London flat. Benedict, surprisingly, seemed to thrive in the bucolic setting. He shed his usual city-slicker attire in favour of borrowed overalls, looking endearingly awkward but undeniably charming in his clumsy attempt at rural chic. We'd rented a charming cottage, all exposed beams and crackling fireplaces, a world away from the minimalist aesthetic of our apartment.

The change of scenery seemed to unlock something within him. The usual sharp edges of his wit were softened, replaced by a gentle curiosity about the natural world. We spent hours walking through sun-dappled fields, his earlier pronouncements on the futility of nature replaced with a quiet appreciation of its beauty. He even, and I still find it hard to believe, helped me weed the cottage garden, his city- slicker hands surprisingly adept at coaxing stubborn weeds from the earth.

One evening, sitting by the fire, a bottle of surprisingly decent local wine between us, the conversation drifted towards our childhoods. It was a rare glimpse into the man behind the carefully constructed persona he'd presented to the world. He spoke of a lonely childhood, a stark contrast to my own privileged upbringing. He described a father consumed by work, a distant figure who never quite understood his son's artistic inclinations. There was a vulnerability in his voice, a rawness that stripped away the layers of sarcasm and wit, revealing a man yearning for connection, for understanding.

I found myself drawn into his story, my own carefully guarded walls beginning to crumble. I spoke of my own disappointments, my own struggles, things I'd never shared with anyone, certainly not with someone I'd initially viewed as a project. It was a risk, a leap of faith, but in the comforting glow of the fireplace, with the wind whispering through the ancient trees outside, it felt natural, inevitable.

The next morning, we woke to a thick blanket of fog, the countryside transformed into a mystical landscape. We walked hand-in-hand, the silence comfortable, intimate. There were no witty retorts, no intellectual sparring, just a shared appreciation of the quiet beauty of the landscape, the unspoken connection between us growing stronger with each shared breath. The fog seemed to erase the boundaries between us, making the unspoken feelings palpable in the crisp morning air.

The following day, we ventured into the nearby village, a picture of quintessential English charm. Benedict, surprisingly, engaged with the locals, his city-bred cynicism replaced with a genuine interest in their lives. He even managed a conversation with the elderly woman who owned the village shop, exchanging pleasantries and a shared chuckle over the notoriously unpredictable British weather. The transformation was complete. The man I had initially set out to "tame" was gone, replaced by someone entirely new, someone genuine, someone real.

That evening, as we sat on the cottage porch, watching the sun dip below the horizon, painting the sky in hues of orange and purple, he confessed to having never truly understood art until he met me. He claimed my approach to life, my sharp wit, my unyielding independence, had provided him with the insight to comprehend the beauty and complexity of his own artistic endeavors.

It was a surprising confession, one that I found deeply moving. His words weren't merely flattery; they were a testament to the unexpected ways in which our lives intertwine, how the seemingly chaotic elements of life often combine to create something beautiful and profound. He had learned from me, not just artistic techniques or social graces, but a deeper understanding of himself, of his potential.

In turn, I confessed that my own rigidly constructed life, my carefully planned existence, had been lacking something fundamental – authenticity. He had challenged me, pushed me beyond my comfort zone, forcing me to confront my own fears, vulnerabilities, and the unexpected stirrings of my own heart. I realized that my attempts to "tame" him had inadvertently set me free. My meticulously crafted life, with its algorithms and spreadsheets, had been a gilded cage, and he had been the key that unlocked it.

The weekend in the countryside wasn't merely a change of scenery; it was a turning point in our relationship. The idyllic setting, the tranquil atmosphere, provided the perfect backdrop for vulnerability and intimacy. We laughed, we cried, we shared our deepest fears and dreams. It was raw, honest, and utterly exhilarating. The sharp wit and playful banter remained, but now there was an underlying layer of warmth, of affection, that transcended the mere intellectual sparring.

It dawned on me that my initial motivations, rooted in a desire for control, were flawed. What I'd thought of as 'taming' was actually a journey of mutual discovery, a shared exploration of two distinct personalities finding common ground, a testament to the unexpected power of human connection. The lines of our relationship, once stark and clearly defined, now blurred, intertwining in a beautiful tapestry of shared experiences and newfound affection.

Returning to London felt different. The city, which had once seemed to represent the calculated aspects of my life, now held a different meaning. It was the stage where our evolving relationship would play out. The city, with its frenetic energy, became a vibrant backdrop to our deepening connection, a silent witness to our growth and transformation. The meticulously planned existence I'd once craved felt unnecessary, even silly. My perfectly curated life felt small, insignificant in comparison to the immensity of our unfolding relationship.

Benedict, transformed and reborn, continued his artistic pursuits with a newfound energy and purpose. His work evolved, reflecting not just his artistic growth but the journey we'd taken together. His abstract expressionism, once chaotic, now incorporated an intriguing sense of harmony, the contrasting elements weaving together in a symphony of color and form, reflecting the complex balance of our evolving relationship.

The initial shock of our unexpected feelings had indeed faded, replaced by something far more profound. It was no longer a carefully constructed experiment; it was a genuine connection, a shared experience, a love story born not from a meticulously planned strategy but from the unplanned, the spontaneous, the utterly beautiful messiness of life. The spreadsheets remained, gathering dust, a monument to a past I no longer recognized. And that, I realized, was a perfect ending in itself. The rain had stopped. The sun was shining. And I knew, with absolute certainty, that this was just the beginning.

FACING THE
UNEXPECTED

The meticulously planned weekend in the Cotswolds, designed to subtly, yet effectively, "refine" Benedict, had been a resounding success – or so I'd thought. He'd emerged from the experience a changed man, his usual cynicism tempered by a newfound appreciation for both nature and, dare I say it, me. But the countryside idyll, with its gentle breezes and picturesque sunsets, couldn't mask the realities of our return to London. The city, with its relentless pace and relentless demands, presented a different kind of challenge, a test of the fragile connection we'd forged amidst the wildflowers and rolling hills.

Our first major hurdle arrived in the form of a rather large, rather hairy, and rather unexpected dog. Benedict, in a moment of spontaneous generosity (a newfound trait, I'll admit), had agreed to dog-sit for his eccentric neighbour, a flamboyant artist known for her equally flamboyant collection of rescue animals. This particular rescue was a behemoth of a Saint Bernard, a creature of immense size and even more immense slobber capacity. His name, fittingly, was Chaos.

Chaos, it turned out, had a penchant for destruction that rivaled my own carefully curated spreadsheets. He'd chewed through Benedict's prized collection of limited-edition art books (a particularly expensive edition of Picasso's sketches, I might add), redecorated the living room with a vibrant assortment of mud, and had a concerning fondness for my Jimmy Choos. My carefully constructed world, with its perfectly organized chaos, was, quite literally, unraveling.

My initial reaction, predictably, was to deploy my usual arsenal of strategic planning. I drew up a detailed schedule, complete with feeding times, walking routes, and a meticulously designed training regimen. Benedict, however, found himself oddly charmed by the canine chaos. He spent hours playing fetch in the park, his carefully tailored suits replaced by old jeans and a thoroughly mud-splattered t- shirt. He even started talking to the dog, engaging in what I could only describe as a profound philosophical discussion about the nature of existential angst.

This blatant disregard for my meticulously planned approach irritated me to no end. My carefully constructed order was being disrupted, my carefully cultivated control being challenged. The initial shock of my unexpected feelings had indeed faded, but they'd been replaced by another surprise: jealousy. Not the irrational, possessive jealousy of the soap opera variety, but a subtle, creeping resentment towards the dog. Chaos, with his clumsy enthusiasm and unwavering devotion, was stealing Benedict's attention, and it was unsettling.

My inner monologue, usually a refined symphony of wit and intellectual prowess, descended into a cacophony of petulant complaints. "He spends more time with that dog than with me," I'd mutter to myself as I painstakingly scrubbed mud from my antique Persian rug. "He should be spending time with me, perfecting his table manners, not discussing Sartre with a slobbering beast!"

The situation reached its peak one evening when Benedict, covered in dog hair and smelling faintly of wet fur, announced his intention to take Chaos on a weekend camping trip. Camping. The very word conjured up images of uncomfortable sleeping bags, questionable hygiene, and a complete absence of my carefully planned itineraries. My carefully constructed composure cracked.

"Are you serious?" I asked, my voice laced with a barely concealed fury.

He looked at me, a mixture of amusement and

concern in his eyes. "It's Chaos. He needs to... experience nature."

"And I need to experience a weekend without a hairy, slobbery, destructive canine tornado!" I retorted. My voice, sharper than I'd intended, echoed through the apartment. The carefully crafted façade of the independent, unflappable woman crumbled in front of his eyes.

He saw past the anger, past the carefully constructed walls I'd built around my heart. He saw the vulnerability, the unexpected insecurity. He came closer, his hand gently brushing a stray strand of hair from my face. "Katherine," he said softly, "I understand."

The unexpected admission silenced me. It was more than an understanding of my annoyance with Chaos; it was an acknowledgement of my own vulnerabilities, my own unexpected need for reassurance. The admission surprised me more than any of his previous actions. His capacity for empathy, for genuine emotional connection, hadn't been part of my initial calculations. He had changed, yes, but so had I.

The camping trip went ahead, of course. I wouldn't let a dog, however destructive, dictate my plans entirely. I reluctantly conceded, but only after devising a detailed itinerary, a comprehensive packing list, and a contingency plan for every possible canine-related emergency. I even packed a miniature first aid kit, complete with antiseptic wipes and tweezers for removing errant burrs from his fur.

That weekend, amidst the chaos of tent pitching, campfire cooking, and unexpected downpours, I found a new kind of connection with Benedict, one that transcended the intellectual sparring and strategic maneuvering. We laughed at the absurd situations that arose, shared moments of quiet contemplation under the starlit sky, and even found ourselves collaborating on a rather abstract artwork using mud and twigs.

The unexpected event – Chaos, the dog – had forced us to confront our own vulnerabilities, and in doing so, strengthened the foundation of our evolving relationship. The carefully crafted plans had served their purpose, but the most profound moments came not from calculated strategies, but from spontaneous acts of connection, from a shared laughter amidst the chaos of life. It was a messy, unexpected, and wonderfully liberating experience. And as the week ended, and we returned to London, it was the messy, unpredictable aspects of our relationship that stood out, the aspects I previously sought to control. The dog? Well, the damage was considerable. But then again, sometimes the best relationships are the ones that leave you happily muddy, and slightly bewildered, at the end of the day. The chaos, it seemed, was only just beginning.

A MOMENT OF TRUTH

The return to London had been, shall we say, less than idyllic. The meticulously planned Cotswolds weekend, designed to subtly – very subtly – hone Benedict's rough edges, had yielded surprisingly positive results. Or so I'd convinced myself. The reality of navigating London life with a newly "refined" Benedict proved to be a far cry from the bucolic charm of the countryside. The city, with its relentless pace and inherent chaos, presented a different kind of test – a test of our evolving, and rather unexpectedly tender, connection.

It wasn't the city itself that posed the most immediate threat, but rather a four-legged, slobbering, and decidedly destructive force of nature named Chaos. Benedict, in a fit of spontaneous generosity (a remarkably new development in his personality), had agreed to dog-sit for his neighbour, a woman whose artistic flair seemed to mirror her questionable judgement in pet selection. Chaos, a Saint Bernard of truly epic proportions, possessed an almost supernatural ability to unravel even the most meticulously organized plans.

My carefully curated apartment, usually a haven of calm and efficiency, transformed into a disaster zone. The pristine white walls bore the markings of muddy paws, my antique Persian rug was now sporting a rather fetching mud-splatter design, and my Jimmy Choo stilettos had clearly become the preferred chew-toy of this canine behemoth. My inner monologue, usually a symphony of witty observations and selfdeprecating humor, descended into a series of increasingly frantic mutterings. "He's destroyed a first edition of Proust!" I wailed to my reflection one particularly

chaotic morning. "Proust! And the dog is wearing my cashmere scarf!"

Benedict, however, seemed utterly charmed by this furry tornado of destruction. He spent hours engaged in philosophical discussions (or at least what appeared to be philosophical discussions) with Chaos, the dog seemingly hanging onto every word with rapt attention. The man who once dismissed emotional displays as overly sentimental was now actively engaged in playful wrestling matches, his impeccably tailored suits replaced by clothes that seemed to attract mud like a magnet. I admit, witnessing his transformation, this newfound connection with a creature of such alarming slobber capacity, ignited a spark of something unexpected within me: Jealousy.

Not the irrational, possessive jealousy often found in cheap romance novels, but a more nuanced, almost perplexing resentment. Chaos, with his clumsy enthusiasm and seemingly boundless adoration, was stealing Benedict's attention. He was usurping my place in the hierarchy of affection, and I found myself struggling with a wave of unforeseen insecurity. The situation reached a fever pitch when Benedict, covered in dog hair and reeking of wet fur, nonchalantly announced his intention to take Chaos on a weekend camping trip.

"Camping?" I exclaimed, my voice sharper than intended. The carefully constructed walls of my composure crumbled. "Are you serious? We're going camping with a dog that has a penchant for destroying priceless possessions?"

He looked at me, his expression a mixture of amusement and genuine concern. "Katherine," he said softly, "He needs to... experience nature." His tone was patient, understanding, a stark contrast to the usual sharp wit I'd come to expect.

"And I," I retorted, "need to experience a weekend free from canineinduced chaos! I have work to do, deadlines to meet! This isn't some whimsical holiday, it's a strategic retreat!

There are plans, Benedict, plans that do not involve sharing a tent with a slobbering Saint Bernard!"

My outburst was both surprising and relieving. The carefully crafted image of the perfectly controlled, unflappable Katherine cracked, revealing a vulnerable woman beneath the surface. I saw a flicker of understanding in his eyes, a recognition of the unexpected emotions churning beneath my carefully maintained exterior. He saw past the anger, the carefully constructed defenses, to the insecure heart beating underneath.

His response was unexpected. Instead of dismissal or the usual sarcastic retort, he came closer, his touch gentle as he brushed a stray strand of hair from my face. "Katherine," he said, his voice low and reassuring, "I understand."

It was more than understanding my annoyance with Chaos. It was an acknowledgement of my vulnerability, my unexpected need for reassurance, a testament to the surprising depth of his empathy. This capacity for genuine emotional connection, this ability to see beyond my carefully constructed facades, had never been part of my carefully laid plans.

The camping trip did, inevitably, go ahead. After all, I wasn't about to let a dog dictate my every move. But the meticulous planning was even more rigorous than usual. I created an itinerary that would make a military strategist proud. A comprehensive packing list that anticipated every possible canine-related emergency, a contingency plan for everything from rogue squirrels to spontaneous rainstorms. I even packed a miniature first-aid kit, complete with antiseptic wipes and tweezers for removing burrs from Chaos's luxurious fur.

The weekend itself proved to be both chaotic and surprisingly fulfilling. The carefully planned itinerary quickly fell by the wayside, replaced by spontaneous laughter, shared moments of quiet contemplation under the starlit sky, and even a surprisingly successful collaborative mudand-twig artwork. We navigated the challenges together – the leaky tent, the soggy marshmallows, Chaos's persistent attempts to eat my meticulously prepared sandwiches – with a newfound sense of camaraderie. Through the laughter and the shared frustrations, I saw a different side of Benedict, a tenderness and vulnerability I hadn't anticipated.

The unexpected event – Chaos, the dog – became a catalyst for a deeper connection. It forced us to confront our vulnerabilities, our unexpected needs for each other. It transcended the calculated strategies and intellectual sparring that had defined our initial interactions, revealing a more genuine, more profound connection. It was messy, unpredictable, and utterly liberating.

The return to London was different. The city seemed less oppressive, less demanding. The chaos of the weekend had somehow prepared us for the everyday chaos of urban life. We had faced the unexpected, the unplanned, and we'd emerged stronger, closer. And as I looked at Benedict, slightly muddy, utterly charming, and completely bewildered by the complexities of our relationship, I realised the 'taming' wasn't about control, but about shared laughter, navigating the chaos together. The unexpected feelings I'd initially dismissed as illogical jealousy had morphed into something profound and irreplaceable. And honestly, I had a sneaking

suspicion that the real chaos was only just beginning. In the best possible way, of course.

CLASH OF PERSONALITIES

The post-camping trip euphoria, however, proved short- lived. The honeymoon period, if one could even call it that, given our perpetually combative dynamic, had a decidedly limited shelf life. The return to our respective routines highlighted the fundamental differences in our personalities, differences that the shared adversity of a leaky tent and a mud-obsessed Saint Bernard had only temporarily masked.

Benedict, for instance, retained his unwavering belief in the power of routine. His mornings were a meticulously orchestrated ballet of precisely timed activities: a precisely measured cup of Earl Grey tea, a precisely allocated 45 minutes for reading the Financial Times (online, of course, because paper cuts were simply inefficient), and a precisely scheduled 30-minute power walk. My mornings, on the other hand, were a chaotic free-for-all, a whirlwind of creative inspiration, lastminute deadlines, and a general sense of controlled pandemonium.

The clash of these two diametrically opposed approaches to life became a daily battleground.

His attempts at incorporating my "chaotic energy" into his structured world resulted in predictable disaster. He once tried to integrate my "creative writing sessions" into his schedule, allotting a specific twohour block for my "word- producing activities." The result? Two hours of crippling self-doubt, writer's block, and a profound sense of creative suffocation. My attempts to introduce spontaneity into his regimented life were equally disastrous. A surprise trip to an impromptu jazz club ended with Benedict looking utterly bewildered amidst the swirling smoke and frenetic energy.

He seemed more traumatized than entertained, murmuring

about the "disruptive auditory stimuli" and the "unpredictable movements of the patrons."

His attempts at incorporating "spontaneity" into his rigid schedule led to equally disastrous results. One memorable occasion involved a supposedly "spontaneous" picnic in Hyde Park. The picnic, meticulously planned down to the last cucumber sandwich, was executed with the precision of a military operation. It involved a detailed map, a pre- determined route, and a comprehensive contingency plan for inclement weather. Spontaneity, it seemed, had been carefully scheduled and tightly controlled. The sheer irony was almost painful. I spent most of the picnic suppressing a laugh, finding the entire charade almost endearing in its misguided attempt to break free from his rigid routine.

The differences extended beyond our daily routines. Our approaches to problem-solving were as different as night and day. Benedict, a creature of logic and reason, favored a methodical, analytical approach. He dissected every issue, weighing every possible outcome with the precision of a surgeon. I, on the other hand, approached problems with a certain amount of chaotic intuition, often leaping to conclusions and relying on gut feeling rather than logical deduction. The resulting friction was frequently explosive, with our contrasting styles frequently leading to heated arguments and intellectual sparring matches.

One particularly memorable argument revolved around the best way to deal with a persistent leak in the bathroom ceiling. Benedict, armed with a toolbox and a wealth of DIY manuals, was determined to fix the leak himself. His approach was methodical, painstaking, and driven by a desire for perfection. He spent hours meticulously dissecting the problem, measuring, calculating, and referring to obscure plumbing diagrams. I, meanwhile, suggested a far more

radical solution: hiring a professional plumber. My reasoning? I was more interested in a dry bathroom than engaging in a potentially catastrophic plumbing adventure with a man who saw a dripping faucet as a personal challenge.

The argument escalated, our voices rising in pitch as we exchanged increasingly exasperated pronouncements on the merits of DIY versus professional expertise. The battle raged on for days, the leaky ceiling becoming a potent symbol of our conflicting approaches to life. The leak, predictably, remained. The plumber, ultimately called in to resolve the matter, fixed the problem in less than an hour, silently observing the aftermath of our intellectual battle with an expression of amused resignation. As he collected his payment, his eyes met mine, and for a moment, we silently acknowledged the absurdity of the situation, the profound disparity between our approaches.

Beyond domestic squabbles, our differences extended to our social lives. Benedict's social circle comprised mostly of equally regimented individuals, a group of high-flying executives and strategically networked professionals. My social landscape, on the other hand, was a vibrant kaleidoscope of artists, musicians, and free spirits. The incompatibility of these worlds was evident during our attempts at shared social engagements. A dinner party I organized, intended to be a vibrant display of creative chaos, left Benedict visibly uncomfortable. The boisterous laughter, the passionate discussions, and the general lack of structured conversation protocol were clearly beyond his comfort zone.

Conversely, a formal dinner at Benedict's golf club left me feeling distinctly out of place among the impeccably dressed members and the polite, yet somewhat sterile, conversations. I found myself desperately searching for an escape,

envisioning a world far removed from the precisely measured wine glasses and the meticulously planned seating arrangements. The inherent clash between our social worlds was clear, a stark contrast between the free-flowing energy of my life and the rigid formality of his.

Despite the constant friction, there were moments of unexpected harmony. These moments were usually punctuated by shared laughter, a mutual recognition of the absurdity of our differences. They were reminders that despite our contrasting personalities, our fundamental connection remained. It was in those moments, in the shared amusement of our everyday struggles, that I saw a glimpse of something deeper, something that transcended the surface level clashes of our personalities. We were learning, slowly and painfully, to appreciate the other's perspective, to acknowledge the value of the contrasting approaches. We were learning, grudgingly but surely, to navigate the complexities of our relationship, appreciating the unique flavor this peculiar partnership brought to our lives. The journey was undoubtedly chaotic, but that chaos, it seemed, was precisely the point. It was messy, illogical, and perpetually unpredictable; yet, beneath the daily battles of personalities, there was a spark, a surprising affection that suggested this unconventional pairing was far from over. The taming, as it turned out, was a two-way street, a continuous, evolving process that involved a whole lot of laughter, a healthy dose of frustration, and a surprising amount of mutual respect. The real challenge, I realised, wasn't about taming the other person, but about taming the expectations and embracing the joyous chaos of an unpredictable love.

LEARNING TO COMPROMISE

The leaky ceiling debacle, as it became affectionately known, served as a pivotal moment. It wasn't just about the dripping water; it was about the fundamental clash in our approaches to life. Benedict, ever the pragmatist, saw it as a technical challenge, a puzzle to be solved with precision and logic. I, ever the pragmatist in my own delightfully chaotic way, saw it as an inconvenience best delegated to someone with more experience than a man who once tried to use a spork to unclog a drain. The argument, while fiery, ultimately led to a grudging acceptance of compromise. Not surrender, mind you, but a strategic retreat – a tactical manoeuvre that would secure us a dry bathroom without sacrificing our respective egos (too much).

He finally agreed to call a plumber, but only after a detailed costbenefit analysis that spanned several spreadsheets. I, in return, agreed to accompany him on his next meticulously planned Saturday morning power walk – provided he didn't attempt to time my breathing pattern or chart my stride length. The concession on my part involved a significant internal struggle, because honestly, the prospect of being subjected to Benedict's hyper-organized physical fitness regimen felt as appealing as a root canal without anesthesia. Yet, the silent acknowledgment, hidden within the shared sigh of exhaustion following the plumber's visit, that we were both capable of relinquishing something important for the sake of a functional bathroom, was profound.

The compromises didn't stop there. His attempts at integrating me into his rigidly structured social life involved a series of carefully curated events. He introduced me to his golf club, but with a crucial twist.
Instead of the stuffy,

formal dinner party, we attended a 'casual' Friday night drinks event – a seemingly contradictory concept to anyone familiar with Benedict's usual social sphere. Even in this "casual" setting, there was a subtle attempt at control; he'd pre-selected our drinks, and the location, a meticulously planned compromise that made it feel a tad less like a high- stakes negotiation and more like a sophisticated game of chess. I, on the other hand, introduced him to the vibrant chaos of my artist friends' loft parties. To his credit, he didn't immediately flee at the sight of abstract art and experimental music, but the faint grimace of a man contemplating a sudden bout of sensory overload was unmistakable.

It was in these seemingly insignificant compromises that the real progress occurred. He learned to appreciate the value of spontaneity, not just as an abstraction, but as an experience. He discovered that a world devoid of perfectly scheduled events was not necessarily a chaotic wasteland, but a vibrant, unpredictable landscape of possibilities. I, in turn, discovered the value of structure, not as a stifling constraint but as a framework for security and stability. We learned that compromise didn't mean surrendering your individuality, but rather, it meant sharing a map, navigating the terrain together. It meant a willingness to venture beyond the familiar, stepping into the other person's world, even if it felt as foreign as a Martian colony.

One evening, amidst the comforting rhythm of a shared cup of tea (his precisely measured portion, my slightly less precise, but equally appreciated, amount), we engaged in a discussion about our ongoing culinary experiments.

Benedict, a master of precise cooking times and ingredient quantities, had attempted to bake a cake according to a strict, scientifically precise recipe, a mathematical equation in the form of a dessert. The result, while technically perfect in terms of texture and density, resembled an edible concrete

slab more than a delectable treat. I, in contrast, had followed a 'whimsical' approach, throwing in a handful of this, a sprinkle of that, guided entirely by instinct and a healthy disregard for precise measurements. My cake resembled something that exploded out of a particularly vivid dream, a vibrant and slightly messy expression of culinary inspiration. He admitted that my slightly chaotic approach, although unorthodox, had yielded a more appealing result. I, in turn, admitted that his precise measurements had, in fact, produced a cake with a texture that was remarkably similar to the smoothness of a fine wine, even if the visual appeal could have used some improvement.

The learning curve was steep, punctuated by the occasional relapse into our old habits. There were times when his penchant for meticulously planned schedules felt suffocating, and times when my bursts of impulsive creativity threatened to destabilize the foundation of our mutual understanding. We stumbled, we bickered, we occasionally threatened to revert to our pre-compromise state of perpetual antagonism. Yet, each time, the shared acknowledgment of our need for mutual respect, the silent understanding that we were both willing to adapt and evolve, cemented our bond. It wasn't about giving up our core identities; it was about expanding our horizons, learning to embrace the differences that ultimately enriched our lives.

Our compromise extended beyond the mundane. We began to incorporate aspects of each other's perspectives into our larger life goals. Benedict, inspired by my creative chaos, started to embrace a certain degree of flexibility in his professional life. He still maintained his meticulous approach, but he found himself incorporating elements of spontaneity, such as brainstorming sessions that diverged from the rigidly structured agendas he previously favored. He discovered that such moments of free-flowing creativity

often led to unexpected breakthroughs, innovative solutions that were never part of his initial, meticulously planned objectives.

I, in turn, began to incorporate some of Benedict's structure into my own chaotic life. Setting deadlines, previously an act of self-torture, became a tool for achieving greater creative output. The act of precisely allocating time for different tasks transformed from a rigid constraint to a productive strategy. It was as if we had become two puzzle pieces, initially clashing in their shapes and sizes, but eventually finding a perfect fit, forming a unique pattern that was both intricate and beautiful.

The taming, as it turned out, wasn't about altering each other's fundamental personalities. It wasn't about forceful conformity or the imposition of one's will on another. It was about learning to coexist, respecting the unique dance of our differences, understanding that the art of partnership was not about creating uniformity, but about celebrating the contrasting notes that created a harmony uniquely our own. It was about finding the space to be ourselves, whilst acknowledging the other's existence, a constant push and pull, a give and take that ultimately resulted in a more profound and fulfilling connection than we could have ever imagined. And it all started with a leaky ceiling, a badly baked cake, and the realization that sometimes, the most satisfying outcome is one that deviates delightfully from the plan.

EXTERNAL CONFLICTS

The initial tentative steps towards a shared existence were, predictably, met with a chorus of raised eyebrows and thinly veiled skepticism from our respective social circles.

Benedict's friends, a collection of impeccably dressed, financially secure individuals who favored predictable routines and even more predictable conversations, viewed my introduction into their carefully curated world with a mixture of polite curiosity and cautious apprehension. The sight of me, clad in a vibrant, mismatched outfit that screamed "artistic rebellion" and holding a half-eaten chocolate éclair, was clearly unsettling. Their perfectly manicured lawns seemed to wilt slightly in my presence.

Their hushed whispers, laced with thinly veiled concern about Benedict's sudden detour from his meticulously planned existence, were almost comical. One particularly daring soul, a woman whose perfectly sculpted hair could have doubled as an architectural marvel, cautiously inquired about my "professional pursuits," her tone suggesting she expected me to be a high-powered lawyer, a successful CEO, or perhaps a curator of some obscure art collection that justified my flamboyance. When I replied, with a perfectly deadpan expression, that I was a professional chaos agent, specializing in the disruption of conventional norms, I could practically feel the collective shudder rippling through their carefully controlled social fabric.

My friends, on the other hand, were equally baffled, but for entirely different reasons. Their initial reaction to Benedict was a mix of bewildered amusement and outright hostility. To them, Benedict was a living embodiment of everything they jokingly referred to as "the patriarchy in a bespoke

suit." His precise manner, his unwavering adherence to schedules, and his tendency to dissect even the most trivial subjects with the analytical precision of a brain surgeon all seemed to clash violently with their bohemian lifestyle. The sight of him attempting to navigate their chaotic art studio, meticulously wiping paint splatters off his impeccably polished shoes, was a source of unending amusement and mockery.

One particularly memorable incident involved Benedict's attempt to participate in a collaborative art project. The project, involving a large canvas, various paint colors and a fair amount of wine, resulted in what can only be described as a scene from an avant-garde circus. Benedict, armed with a ruler, a protractor, and a color chart, attempted to create a symmetrical masterpiece while everyone else wielded brushes with the reckless abandon of people who knew that perfection was the enemy of art. The result, a chaotic blend of clashing colors and geometric shapes, was eventually declared "a bold commentary on the tension between order and chaos in modern society," though privately, my friends suspected that it was just a drunken accident.

Beyond the social circles, unexpected obstacles kept presenting themselves. A significant challenge arose when Benedict's meticulous budgeting clashed with my spontaneous spending habits. While he meticulously tracked every penny, meticulously planning for long-term investments and financial security, my approach to finance was, shall we say, less systematic. A sudden impulse to buy an antique typewriter, or a vintage kimono, or a trip to Italy to "find myself" (and maybe some particularly delicious gelato) would throw his carefully constructed spreadsheets into disarray. His attempts at "financial education" consisted of hour-long lectures that usually ended with me giggling uncontrollably, my attention wandering towards the more compelling allure of the cat videos on my phone.

The challenges extended beyond the financial

sphere. Benedict's unwavering belief in the importance of punctuality created a persistent source of friction. My perception of time was more fluid, guided less by clocks and calendars and more by inspiration, a sense of intuition that rarely aligned with the precisely calculated schedules that ruled Benedict's life. Our attempts at attending social events together were often marred by my habitual lateness, a detail that caused Benedict much angst and internal turmoil.

Interestingly, these external conflicts, instead of tearing us apart, served as a crucible for our relationship. They forced us to confront our differences not as insurmountable obstacles, but as unique perspectives that could enrich and challenge our understanding of each other. The skeptical stares of his friends, initially a source of annoyance, eventually became a source of amusement. We found ourselves laughing at the irony of their disapproval, realizing that our differences were what made our connection so unique. The chaotic art projects became a symbol of our ability to embrace the beautiful messiness of life together.

Even the financial disagreements, while initially frustrating, helped us to learn more about each other's values and priorities.

The journey of compromise wasn't always smooth. There were heated arguments, moments of frustration, and occasions when we both retreated into our respective comfort zones, tempted to surrender to our ingrained habits. But each time, we returned to our shared understanding, acknowledging the need for mutual respect and adaptability. We found ourselves learning to laugh at our differences, even to appreciate the absurdity of our clashing personalities,

to appreciate the beauty of a shared existence crafted from two distinct world views.

Through these external challenges, we redefined the meaning of compromise. It wasn't about abandoning our core identities; it was about recognizing the value of mutual understanding, the importance of respecting differences, the richness of a life lived on the boundaries of contrasting worlds. The external conflicts, once perceived as threats, became catalysts for growth, sharpening our individuality while simultaneously solidifying the foundations of our shared existence. The "taming," as it finally became clear, wasn't about changing one another, but about embracing the unpredictable dance of differences, creating a harmony that transcended the limitations of our individual worlds. And that, perhaps, was the most beautiful and unexpected result of all. The leaky ceiling, the disastrous cake, the bewildered friends and family – these were merely stepping stones on the path to a shared understanding, a testament to the fact that the most fulfilling partnerships are often built on the foundation of delightful, and occasionally chaotic, compromise.

NAVIGATING EXPECTATIONS

The societal pressure, a silent, insidious beast, began to rear its head. It wasn't just our friends and family; it was the pervasive societal narrative whispering its expectations into our ears, a constant low hum of disapproval against the backdrop of our unconventional union. Benedict, bless his meticulously organized heart, found himself grappling with the unspoken expectations placed upon men in the 21st century. He was expected to be the provider, the steady rock, the unwavering pillar of strength, the silent, supportive partner. The traditional role, albeit subtly nuanced for a modern context, still clung to him like a second skin, a legacy of upbringing and ingrained societal programming.

He struggled, bless him, with the subtle barbs and raised eyebrows he received when I, quite deliberately, declined to neatly fit into the role of the "supportive wife." My career, a chaotic yet rewarding whirlwind of freelance writing and artistic collaborations, didn't exactly align with the image of a woman comfortably nestled in a domestic sphere. His discomfort wasn't born from malice, but rather from a deeply ingrained societal conditioning that struggled to reconcile my fiercely independent spirit with the conventional expectation of a "wife." He'd even attempt to subtly "adjust" my schedule, suggesting that I attend a certain networking event or prioritize a particular writing opportunity based on what he perceived as more "suitable" for a partner in *his* world. It was endearing, in its clumsy, well-intentioned way, but ultimately frustrating.

My own struggles were different, yet equally challenging. The expectation placed upon women—to be nurturing, compliant, and perpetually understanding —felt like a

straightjacket. I found myself battling the insidious pressure to conform to a specific image, an image that I had consciously rejected. The expectations were subtly, almost invisibly communicated, through everything from the casual comments of acquaintances to the subtext of articles and advertisements that painted a picture of domestic bliss that felt anything but liberating. People, well-meaning but nonetheless clueless, often approached me with a condescending tone, questioning my choices, suggesting that I should "settle down," or "focus on more important things"—as if my life choices were somehow less valid because they deviated from the conventional script.

One particularly galling instance involved

a family gathering, a meticulously planned affair punctuated by hushed whispers and pointed glances. Benedict's aunt, a woman whose life seemed defined by perfectly arranged floral displays and a suffocating adherence to tradition, felt compelled to comment on my supposed lack of "domestic skills." She was genuinely perplexed by my inability, or rather my unwillingness, to knit, to bake exquisite pastries, to engage in the rituals of polite feminine behavior. This was not out of a desire to offend, but rather a manifestation of her deeply entrenched worldview—one where a woman's worth was measured by her proficiency in traditionally feminine pursuits.

I responded, naturally, with a sarcastic quip about my impressive ability to wield a soldering iron, an answer which only served to reinforce her bewilderment. The underlying current of judgment, however veiled, was palpable. The subtle power dynamics of the situation, the unspoken assumptions, were a constant reminder of the invisible barriers we were navigating. These were not overt acts of aggression; they were the quiet, insidious whispers of

societal expectation, the weight of tradition quietly pressing down.

Even our friends, despite their initial amusement at our unconventional pairing, struggled to reconcile our relationship with their preconceived notions. Benedict's friends, despite their progressive leanings, still held an underlying expectation of a traditional relationship dynamic. They'd often subtly inquire about the division of labor in our household, raising an eyebrow at my admission that the concepts of "his" and "hers" were largely irrelevant to us.

My friends, while accepting of Benedict's eccentricities, occasionally expressed concern about his inherent orderliness, hinting that he might be "too much" for my chaotic spirit.

These were not malicious judgments; they were simply a reflection of the deeply entrenched societal narratives we all, to some extent, internalized. The insidious nature of these expectations lay in their subtle, almost invisible, presence.

They were not explicit demands; they were unspoken assumptions, subtle nudges, the silent pressure to conform. And the challenge lay in navigating these expectations, in forging our own path, while simultaneously acknowledging the inherent complexities of the societal narratives we were up against.

One evening, amidst a particularly challenging conversation with
Benedict's mother about the "proper" way to host a dinner party (apparently, my vibrant, mismatched tableware was considered an affront to good taste), a realization dawned

on us. We weren't just battling societal expectations; we were redefining them. Our relationship, far from being a mere experiment in challenging norms, was a testament to the possibility of forging a partnership built on mutual

respect, shared values, and a conscious rejection of pre-ordained roles.

The fight against societal expectations wasn't about winning; it was about redefining the game. It was about creating a space where our individualities could flourish without compromising our commitment to each other. It was about dismantling the rigid structures that dictated the parameters of relationships, the implicit hierarchies that placed limitations on our individual choices. This wasn't simply about our personal relationship; it was about participating in a larger conversation on the evolution of gender roles and the complexities of modern relationships.

This realization brought a sense of defiant joy. We were not simply navigating expectations; we were actively reshaping them. The challenges we faced became opportunities for growth, for selfdiscovery, for reaffirming our commitment to a relationship built on authenticity rather than conformity. The subtle barbs, the raised eyebrows, even the poorly disguised disapproval – they became badges of honor, testament to the unconventional path we had chosen. We laughed, we argued, we learned, and above all, we adapted, not just to each other, but to the evolving landscape of expectations surrounding us. Our relationship, a unique blend of order and chaos, became a powerful statement against the tyranny of conformity, a vibrant testament to the beauty of unexpected alliances, and a defiant dance against the silent whispers of societal pressure. We were not trying to fit into a pre-defined mold; we were creating our own, a mold that was uniquely ours, beautiful in its imperfections, and strong in its defiance. The journey continued, as messy and wonderful as it always had been, a testament to the enduring power of love in the face of societal pressure. And that, I realized, was a story worth telling.

A STEP FORWARD

The realization that we weren't simply navigating societal expectations but actively reshaping them became a turning point. It wasn't a sudden epiphany, but a gradual dawning, a quiet understanding that bloomed amidst the chaos of our daily lives. One rainy Tuesday, while wrestling with a particularly stubborn paragraph in my latest manuscript – a feminist reimagining of *Beowulf* , naturally – Benedict surprised me. He didn't offer to make me tea, a gesture which would have once been considered a concession to "traditional" gender roles, and which I would have found both endearing and subtly infuriating. Instead, he sat beside me, a mug of strong black coffee warming his hands, and listened. He listened to my frustrations, my anxieties, the sheer frustration of trying to wrangle a narrative that stubbornly refused to cooperate. He didn't offer solutions, didn't attempt to fix the problem, just listened, his presence a quiet anchor in the storm of my creativity. That, I realised, was a step forward.

This seemingly small act resonated deeply. It wasn't about him abandoning his innate orderliness or me suppressing my chaotic nature; it was about mutual respect, about acknowledging the validity of each other's experiences, even when those experiences didn't neatly align with societal expectations. He understood, finally, that my "messiness" wasn't a personal failing, but a fundamental aspect of my creative process, a vital element of my being. And I, in turn, began to truly understand the source of his need for order, his desire to create structure in a world that often felt overwhelming.

It wasn't a sudden shift, a dramatic transformation. It was more of a slow, steady evolution, a gradual adjustment in our perspective, a shared understanding that grew organically from our shared experiences. We learned to communicate more effectively, to articulate our needs and expectations without resorting to the silent language of resentment or passive aggression. We learned to listen, truly listen, to each other, rather than merely waiting for our turn to speak. We practiced the art of empathy, of stepping into each other's shoes, even if those shoes were wildly different in style and size.

This newfound understanding extended beyond our personal dynamic. We started consciously challenging the subtle biases we had both absorbed, unpacking the societal narratives that influenced our perceptions and expectations. It was a daunting task, an ongoing process of deconstruction and reconstruction, of dismantling internalized prejudices and rebuilding our understanding of relationships. We discussed it openly, sometimes with humour, often with surprising vulnerability, acknowledging the complexities of ingrained societal conditioning and the pervasive influence of unconscious bias.

One evening, whilst perusing a particularly egregious article celebrating the supposed "triumph" of women achieving a work-life balance (an oxymoron if ever I heard one), Benedict pointed out the inherent sexism in the piece. His critique wasn't born from a defensive position, but rather from a genuine desire to understand the inequalities embedded in the societal narrative. He even suggested we write a satirical response, a hilarious takedown of the article's naive assumptions. The resulting collaborative piece, a scathing yet humorous indictment of the unrealistic expectations placed upon working mothers, went viral,

unexpectedly becoming a rallying cry for women who felt similarly suffocated by these unrealistic ideals.

This collaborative effort wasn't just a creative outlet; it was a symbolic representation of our evolving relationship. It showcased our ability to work together, to leverage our individual strengths to create something larger than ourselves, a testament to the power of a partnership based on mutual respect and shared intellectual curiosity. It also showed us the potential to use our shared voice to challenge societal norms, to disrupt the established narrative, and to contribute to a broader conversation on gender roles and relationships.

Our growth wasn't without its bumps, its moments of frustration, its disagreements. There were still times when Benedict's inherent orderliness clashed with my creative chaos, times when my outspoken nature irritated his need for peace and quiet. But the difference was that now, these conflicts were navigated with greater understanding and a shared commitment to mutual respect. We had learned to disagree without being disagreeable, to communicate our needs effectively, and to compromise without compromising our individual identities.

One particularly significant compromise involved Benedict's meticulously planned Saturday mornings. He had a precise schedule – a detailed itinerary, if you will – that involved a specific sequence of activities, each timed down to the minute. It included things like precisely timed tea preparation, a silent period of reflection, and the meticulous organization of his sock drawer. For a time, I had been a reluctant participant, feeling like an outsider trying to navigate the rigid parameters of his ritualistic Saturday.

However, instead of railing against the structure, I attempted to understand it. I realized it wasn't about control, but about comfort, about creating a sense of order in his life. So, we compromised. I suggested a slight adjustment to his timetable, adding a space for our own shared activity: a brisk walk in the park, a shared breakfast, or a spontaneous creative collaboration.

The compromise was a testament to our evolving understanding. It wasn't about one of us conceding, but about creating a space where both our needs could be met. It was a lesson in the art of negotiation, a recognition that compromise doesn't equate to surrender, but rather to a shared construction of a common ground.

Our journey was far from over. The societal whispers still echoed, the expectations still pressed down. But now, we faced them armed with a newfound understanding, a shared conviction, and the ability to navigate the challenges with resilience, humor, and a fierce determination to forge our own path, a path that defied the constraints of traditional gender roles and celebrated the unique beauty of our unconventional union.

It was a long road, full of laughter and tears, of compromises and compromises made and broken, of arguments and reconciliations. But it was a road we were traversing together, hand-in-hand, side-by-side, creating our own map as we went. And that, I realized, was the most rewarding adventure of all –

not just in navigating the complexities of a modern relationship, but in challenging the very definition of what that relationship could be. The challenge wasn't in conforming to an outdated script, but in rewriting the narrative, one chapter, one compromise, one shared laugh at a time. It was about creating a love story that was uniquely ours, a defiant testament to the beauty of imperfection, and the resilience of a love that dared to challenge convention.

The story was still unfolding, a vibrant, evolving tapestry of

laughter, tears, and unwavering commitment. And I, for one, couldn't wait to see what the next chapter would bring. The journey, it seemed, was the real destination. And it was a journey I was thrilled to be sharing with Benedict, a man who, in his own meticulously ordered way, had learned to embrace the delightful chaos of loving a woman who refused to be tamed.

EMBRACING IMPERFECTIONS

The rain outside had intensified, a relentless drumming against the windowpanes that mirrored the tempestuous emotions swirling within me. Benedict, ever the pragmatist, had retreated to his meticulously organized study, leaving me grappling with the messy aftermath of a particularly heated argument. It wasn't a fight about anything significant, not really. It was the usual dance of clashing personalities – his need for order, my embrace of controlled chaos. This time, however, the friction had ignited a spark of self-reflection. I realized that my resistance to his need for order wasn't simply a clash of personalities, but a deep-seated fear. A fear of losing myself in his structured world, a fear of being absorbed, of my vibrant, chaotic essence being stifled by his neat compartments.

And then it hit me – the core of the issue wasn't his orderliness, but my own insecurity. I had built a persona, a shield of sarcastic wit and defiant independence, to protect myself from vulnerability, from the fear of being truly seen. My carefully cultivated messiness was, in a twisted way, a comfort zone. It was a way of keeping people at arm's length, a barrier against intimacy. Benedict, with his quiet understanding and steadfast patience, was slowly chipping away at that carefully constructed facade. He was showing me, not telling me, that it was okay to be imperfect, to be vulnerable, to be... messy.

He reappeared, not with an apology, but with a steaming mug of chamomile tea and a plate of ridiculously decadent chocolate brownies. "My apologies for the earlier outburst," he said, his voice a soft counterpoint to the storm outside. "My need for order can sometimes manifest in rather...

controlling ways." His self-awareness surprised me, a stark contrast to the usual polite but firm dismissal of my complaints. He was acknowledging his flaws, not deflecting or justifying them. It was a radical act of vulnerability in itself.

"And my chaos, in turn, can sometimes feel like a tidal wave of utter disregard for schedules," I replied, a hesitant smile playing on my lips. The tension began to ease, the storm clouds parting, revealing a sliver of sunshine between us.

The brownies were delicious, rich and intensely chocolatey – a perfect counterpoint to the soothing chamomile tea.

We spent the rest of the evening in companionable silence, each absorbed in our own pursuits yet bound together by a shared sense of peace. He quietly reorganized his bookshelves, the rhythmic click of the books a soothing soundtrack to my own quiet contemplation. The rain eventually subsided, leaving behind the soft scent of petrichor and the quiet hum of a contented contentment. I realised that the essence of acceptance wasn't about abandoning our individual traits, but about appreciating them in the context of our relationship. His orderliness wasn't a flaw, but a strength, a source of stability in my occasionally chaotic existence. And my messiness, my creative chaos, wasn't something to be ashamed of, but something to be celebrated – a vibrant expression of my own unique personality.

The following week brought with it a renewed sense of intimacy, an understanding that extended beyond mere tolerance. It was a profound acceptance of our differences, a celebration of our imperfections. We laughed more, argued less, and discovered a new level of vulnerability in our communication. We learned to articulate our needs, not as demands, but as expressions of our individual selves. I

started to see the humor in his meticulous organization, the underlying practicality that fueled his need for control. And he, in turn, seemed to appreciate the vibrant energy, the boundless creativity, and the occasional spectacular mess that was my life.

One Saturday, he surprised me by announcing he had canceled his usual schedule. He had simply declared, "Today, we improvise." This declaration, once unimaginable, represented the monumental shift in our relationship. We spent the day exploring a local antique market, laughing over ludicrously overpriced teacups and arguing about the merits of vintage vinyl. We ended the day by cooking a disastrous but hilarious paella – a culinary testament to our combined, chaotic talents – and watching a bad movie, laughing until our sides ached.

The imperfections weren't erased; they were simply woven into the rich tapestry of our relationship, adding texture, depth, and a unique, irrepressible charm. My chaotic energy complemented his structured routine, creating a dynamic equilibrium. His practicality balanced my impulsive creativity. His quiet contemplation provided a counterpoint to my verbal exuberance. Our differences, once a source of conflict, became our greatest strengths, enriching our lives and deepening our connection.

There were moments, of course, when old habits resurfaced. There were times when his meticulousness grated on my nerves, times when my spontaneous plans disrupted his carefully orchestrated schedule. But now, instead of reacting defensively, we paused, we breathed, and we talked. We communicated honestly and openly, without judgment or resentment. We learned to compromise, not by surrendering our individual identities, but by finding common ground, by understanding the needs and motivations behind our actions.

We even created a shared calendar, a carefully planned but flexible schedule that incorporated both his need for structure and my need for spontaneity. He added buffer zones for "creative chaos," while I agreed to schedule in "orderly moments" – a compromise that felt less like a surrender and more like a playful collaboration. It wasn't simply a calendar; it was a symbol of our evolving relationship, a testament to our willingness to meet each other halfway.

We started to confront some of the deeper societal pressures that had unconsciously shaped our individual perceptions of relationships. We challenged the traditional gender roles that had subtly informed our behaviors, unpacking the assumptions and expectations that had been imposed upon us. It wasn't easy; it required honest self-reflection and a willingness to confront our own biases and insecurities.

The realization that these biases weren't just external forces, but deeply ingrained societal constructs, was a profound and humbling experience. We began to actively challenge these societal norms, both individually and collaboratively. We wrote articles, participated in discussions, and even organized a small community event to promote a more inclusive and understanding approach to relationships. The act of challenging these norms wasn't about rebellion for the sake of it, but rather a desire for genuine connection, a yearning for a relationship that transcended the outdated expectations of society.

And so, our journey continued, evolving and adapting with each passing day. The laughter still echoed, the arguments still simmered, but they were now seasoned with understanding, respect, and a shared appreciation for the unique blend of order and chaos that defined our relationship. The imperfections were no longer flaws; they were the vibrant colours that painted the rich tapestry of our unconventional love story. It wasn't a perfect relationship, not by a long shot. But it was authentic, it was real, and it was uniquely ours – a testament to the transformative power of acceptance and understanding, the beauty of embracing the imperfections, and the joyful chaos of a love that dared to defy convention. The story, I knew, was far from over, but it was a story I was thrilled to continue writing, one imperfectly perfect chapter at a time.

FORGIVENESS AND EMPATHY

The following weeks unfolded like a slow-motion replay of our past arguments, but with a crucial difference: a soundtrack of empathy. It wasn't a magical transformation; the initial friction still existed, the clash of personalities still sparked, but now there was a conscious effort, a deliberate choice to understand rather than react. Benedict's meticulously planned evenings still sometimes collided with my spontaneous bursts of creativity, but instead of a silent standoff or a simmering argument, we found ourselves engaging in a surprisingly enjoyable negotiation. It started with small concessions – me agreeing to a pre-dinner walk instead of a last-minute dash to a gallery opening, him accepting my suggestion of a spontaneous picnic in the park instead of his carefully planned dinner party.

One evening, the argument wasn't avoided. It revolved, predictably, around his insistence on colour-coded spice racks. "Benedict," I sighed, "it's turmeric, not a precious gemstone. It doesn't need its own velvetlined compartment." He looked at me, not with his usual polite defensiveness, but with a hint of genuine amusement. "You're right, of course. It's absurd, isn't it?" He laughed, a genuine, unforced laugh, and together we rearranged the spices, a collaborative effort that dissolved the tension more effectively than any carefully crafted apology.

The act of forgiving each other's past missteps wasn't a grand gesture; it was a series of small, conscious choices. It began with the simple act of listening, truly listening, without interruption or judgment. I discovered that beneath Benedict's need for order lay a deep-seated fear of chaos, a fear stemming from a childhood filled with unpredictable

events. He, in turn, learned that my seeming disregard for schedules stemmed not from a lack of respect, but from an innate creativity that thrived on spontaneity, a creativity that had been suppressed for years under the weight of societal expectations.

This understanding, this empathetic glimpse into each other's pasts, fostered a profound respect for our individual vulnerabilities. We started sharing our insecurities, our fears, not as weaknesses to be hidden but as facets of ourselves to be understood and accepted. I confessed my fear of being perceived as frivolous, of my chaotic energy being dismissed as a lack of seriousness. He admitted his fear of being perceived as controlling, of his need for order being misinterpreted as a lack of flexibility. These confessions, these moments of shared vulnerability, became the bedrock of our evolving relationship.

We learned to identify our respective triggers, the subtle cues that signaled an impending argument. His jaw clenching, my sarcastic tone escalating. These triggers, once sources of conflict, became signals for pause, for reflection, for a conscious effort to de-escalate. Instead of escalating, we took a breath, re-evaluated the situation, and chose empathy over reaction. It wasn't always easy, and there were slip-ups, moments when old habits reasserted themselves, when defensiveness crept in. But each time, we returned to our commitment to understanding, to forgiveness, to empathy.

One Sunday, while strolling through a bustling farmer's market, I caught sight of a woman struggling with overflowing shopping bags. Without hesitation, I rushed to help, remembering my own past struggles balancing work, life and everything in between. Benedict, witnessing my act of kindness, smiled softly. "That's my Katherine," he murmured, his eyes filled with a deep affection. It was in

those quiet moments, those shared gestures of empathy, that the true depth of our connection revealed itself.

The empathy extended beyond our immediate relationship. We began volunteering at a local homeless shelter, an experience that broadened our perspective and deepened our sense of shared purpose. It was in the shared acts of service, the collective effort to alleviate suffering, that our empathy grew even stronger. We saw the struggles of others, their vulnerabilities, their resilience, and it reinforced our commitment to understanding and compassion, both in our relationship and beyond.

Forgiveness, we discovered, was not about forgetting; it was about acknowledging past hurts, acknowledging the mistakes, and choosing to move forward, to build a future grounded in understanding and mutual respect. It wasn't about condoning hurtful actions, but about acknowledging that those actions stemmed from a place of insecurity, from a flawed understanding, rather than malicious intent.

One evening, over a rather disastrous attempt at homemade pasta, Benedict confessed a past mistake, a transgression that had haunted him for years. He spoke with a vulnerability that surprised me, his usually composed exterior cracking to reveal a depth of remorse I hadn't anticipated. My response wasn't judgment, but a quiet acceptance, a shared understanding of the imperfections that make us human. It was a turning point, a moment when the past ceased to cast a shadow on our present.

This journey of forgiveness and empathy wasn't linear; it wasn't a smooth, uninterrupted path. There were bumps, there were detours, there were moments of frustration, doubt and even anger. But through it all, we had each other, our

shared commitment to understanding providing a steady anchor amidst the waves of emotion.

Our relationship evolved, transforming from a delicate dance of clashing personalities into a rich tapestry woven with shared experiences, mutual respect, and a deep, abiding love that embraced both order and chaos. It was a testament to the power of forgiveness, the depth of empathy, and the transformative potential of a relationship built on acceptance and understanding. The rain had long since stopped, and the sun shone brightly on our slightly chaotic, beautifully imperfect life. The ending, as they say, is yet to be written, but the chapters written so far were full of laughter, understanding, and the profound comfort of knowing we were facing the storms together. And that, I realized, was a love story worth telling.

MUTUAL RESPECT

The turning point arrived, not with a grand gesture or a dramatic declaration, but with a shared silence during a particularly disastrous attempt at making sourdough bread. Benedict, ever the meticulous planner, had consulted a dozen online recipes, meticulously measured ingredients, and followed each instruction with the precision of a brain surgeon. Yet, the result was a dense, inedible brick that stubbornly refused to rise. We stared at it, a monument to our combined culinary ineptitude, and instead of the usual volley of sarcastic remarks, a comfortable silence settled between us. It wasn't an awkward silence; it was a shared understanding, a quiet acknowledgement of our fallibility, our shared humanity.

He finally broke the silence, a wry smile playing on his lips. "Perhaps," he conceded, "some things are best left to the professionals." I laughed, a genuine, unrestrained laugh, the kind that comes from a place of deep comfort and shared amusement. It was in that moment, amidst the wreckage of a failed sourdough loaf, that the true depth of our mutual respect solidified. It wasn't about his relinquishing control, or my abandoning my rebellious spirit; it was about accepting each other's imperfections, our shared capacity for both brilliance and utter buffoonery.

This newfound respect wasn't merely about avoiding arguments; it was about navigating disagreements with grace and understanding. We learned to articulate our needs, not as demands, but as requests, acknowledging the other person's perspective even when we disagreed. An evening out, once a battleground of conflicting preferences, became a collaborative exploration of possibilities. He learned to

appreciate my spontaneous whims, understanding that my unpredictable nature wasn't a personal attack, but a reflection of my vibrant creativity. I, in turn, learned to value his need for structure, recognizing that his meticulous planning wasn't about controlling me but about creating a sense of order and comfort in his own life.

This wasn't a sudden, effortless transformation. The old patterns resurfaced occasionally, the echoes of past battles still resonating. There were times when his need for order felt suffocating, when my impulsive actions felt disrespectful. There were moments of frustration, when the old habits of defensiveness and blame threatened to overwhelm our progress. But the difference was significant; we now possessed a shared vocabulary of empathy, a mutual understanding that allowed us to navigate these moments with a newfound maturity.

Instead of escalating conflicts, we sought to understand the root causes of our disagreements. We learned to identify our triggers, to recognize the subtle signals of impending arguments – the tightening of his jaw, the sharpness in my tone – and to consciously choose a different response. We learned to pause, to take a breath, to reframe the situation, to approach the conflict not as an adversarial battle but as a shared problem to be solved. It wasn't about eliminating conflict, because that would be utterly unrealistic; it was about transforming how we approached it.

The impact of this mutual respect extended beyond our personal relationship. We found ourselves working more effectively as a team on professional projects, our complementary skills seamlessly integrating. His methodical approach, coupled with my imaginative flair, resulted in projects that surpassed either of our individual capabilities.

This shared success further strengthened the foundation of

our mutual respect, demonstrating the synergy that resulted from a balanced partnership.

One Saturday morning, whilst browsing a secondhand bookshop, I stumbled across a first edition of a Virginia Woolf novel I'd been searching for, a treasure I knew Benedict would appreciate. The sheer joy of that discovery, the anticipation of his delight, was an unexpected demonstration of my growing affection. It wasn't a grand romantic gesture, rather a subtle act mirroring the quiet understanding that had blossomed between us. His appreciation, expressed not with flowery words but with a shared, knowing smile, was equally potent. These small gestures, the thoughtful acts, were a quiet testament to the depth of our evolving relationship.

This wasn't just about accepting differences; it was about celebrating them. We learned to appreciate the unique perspectives each of us brought to the relationship, recognizing that our contrasting personalities enriched our lives. His methodical approach provided a counterpoint to my impulsive nature, grounding me and preventing me from being swept away by my own chaotic energy. My spontaneity, in turn, injected life and excitement into his meticulously planned world, reminding him to embrace the unexpected joys of life.

This evolution extended beyond our immediate circle; our mutual respect became apparent to our friends and family. The once-strained interactions with his family transformed into genuine connections, fueled by a shared understanding and respect for both our individual needs and our collective happiness. His family, initially apprehensive about my unconventional lifestyle, began to appreciate my unique contributions to his life, recognizing the love and respect underpinning our relationship.

The respect was also visible in the way we managed household chores, no longer a source of passive-aggressive skirmishes but a shared responsibility, each of us contributing based on our individual strengths and preferences. He, with his meticulous nature, tackled the more organized tasks, while I happily took on the more creative endeavors, resulting in a home that reflected both of our individual tastes and our collaborative efforts. The division of labour became a testament to our mutual respect, proving that equality isn't about doing everything equally, but about contributing equitably.

The change wasn't simply a change of behaviour; it was a fundamental shift in perspective, a transformation from a dynamic of dominance and submission to one of genuine partnership. It wasn't about conquering or being conquered; it was about forging a bond built on mutual respect, understanding, and a shared commitment to mutual growth. The "taming" had ceased to be a battle of wills, becoming instead a shared journey of discovery, a testament to the transformative power of empathy and understanding within a relationship.

One evening, as we sat by the fire, sharing a quiet moment of contemplation after a day spent volunteering at a local animal shelter, Benedict looked at me with eyes filled with a deep affection, not the possessive gaze of a man seeking to control, but the warm, appreciative look of a man deeply in love with his equal. The initial spark, that initial clash of personalities, had been refined, honed, and transformed into something far richer and more profound. The "taming" had ultimately led to a mutual respect that transcended the initial premise, showcasing the beauty and complexity of a relationship built on understanding and a genuine appreciation for the other person's inherent worth. And that,

I realised, was a far more satisfying conclusion than any carefully planned, predictable ending. The journey, with all its twists and turns, its arguments and reconciliations, its shared successes and failures, had proven to be the story itself, a testament to the power of mutual respect in a relationship built on love, laughter and a healthy dose of pragmatism. The 'taming' had, in its unexpected way, tamed us both, shaping us into a couple far stronger and more deeply connected than either of us could have ever imagined. The final chapter remained unwritten, but the story, I felt, was finally coming into its own.

FINDING COMMON GROUND

Our shared culinary catastrophe, it turned out, was merely the first domino in a chain reaction of discoveries. The quiet understanding forged amidst the sourdough debacle extended into unexpected realms. Benedict, initially resistant to anything remotely resembling spontaneity, found himself unexpectedly captivated by my impulsive decision to attend a weekend pottery class. He'd envisioned a quiet weekend at home, meticulously planned down to the minute, but he couldn't deny the infectious enthusiasm radiating from me as I described the possibilities of wheel-thrown ceramics. To my surprise, and his own apparent bewilderment, he found himself enjoying the messy, unpredictable nature of the process. The thrill of creating something tangible, something imperfect yet beautiful, resonated with him in a way I hadn't anticipated. It wasn't just about the pottery; it was about sharing an experience, embracing the unexpected joy of learning something new together.

This unexpected shared passion opened up a whole new dimension to our relationship. It wasn't just about conquering our differences; it was about celebrating our similarities, discovering a common ground that transcended our initial clash of personalities. We discovered a shared love for classic literature, spending countless evenings discussing the nuances of Shakespeare, the wit of Austen, and the haunting prose of Woolf. His analytical mind brought a new layer of understanding to the texts, while my intuitive interpretations added a touch of imaginative flair. Our discussions were not simply intellectual exercises; they were passionate explorations, fuelled by a mutual admiration for storytelling and a shared desire to delve deeper into the human condition.

Beyond literature, we discovered a shared fascination with historical architecture. Weekend trips to explore crumbling castles and majestic cathedrals became a recurring theme, our shared appreciation for history and aesthetics forging a stronger connection. These weren't just sightseeing trips; they were journeys of discovery, each building telling a story, each stone whispering tales of the past. We'd linger for hours, examining intricate details, debating historical interpretations, our conversations a blend of historical fact and imaginative speculation. The shared experience, the joint quest for understanding, bound us together in a way that went beyond the superficial.

Our shared interests extended even to the seemingly mundane. We discovered a mutual love for long walks in the countryside, our conversations meandering as freely as the path we walked. These walks weren't merely physical exercise; they were opportunities for introspection, for sharing thoughts and feelings, for letting the rhythms of nature soothe our souls. The quiet intimacy of these walks, the shared silence punctuated by insightful observations, became a cornerstone of our evolving relationship.

These shared passions, these unexpected points of connection, helped to build a solid foundation for our future together. They weren't mere hobbies; they were expressions of our shared values, our shared humanity. The pottery class, the literary discussions, the historical explorations – these were not merely activities; they were the building blocks of a deeper, more meaningful relationship. They represented our growing understanding, our capacity to appreciate each other's strengths, and our willingness to step outside our comfort zones, embracing the unexpected joys that life offered.

The transformation wasn't always seamless; there were still moments of friction, of clashing personalities. But these moments were now approached with a newfound maturity, a shared understanding that allowed us to navigate them with grace and empathy. The disagreements, once fueled by defensiveness and blame, were now addressed with a conscious effort to understand the root causes, to communicate needs and expectations, and to arrive at a mutually agreeable solution. The focus shifted from winning an argument to finding common ground, from asserting dominance to fostering collaboration.

We learned to value each other's strengths, acknowledging that our contrasting personalities weren't obstacles to overcome, but complementary elements that enriched our lives. His methodical approach provided a much-needed counterpoint to my impulsive nature, grounding me and preventing me from being swept away by my own chaotic energy. My spontaneous whims, in turn, injected life and excitement into his meticulously planned world, reminding him to embrace the unexpected joys of life. This dynamic interplay, this harmonious blend of order and chaos, became the defining characteristic of our relationship.

This newfound equilibrium extended beyond our personal lives. We found ourselves working more effectively as a team on professional projects, our complementary skills synergistically enhancing each other's contributions. His meticulous attention to detail combined with my creative vision resulted in projects that surpassed either of our individual capabilities. This shared success further solidified our bond, proving that a true partnership transcends individual ambition, embracing a collaborative spirit that values mutual achievement.

Even mundane tasks, once a source of contention, became opportunities for collaborative effort. Household chores, once a battleground of passive-aggressive skirmishes, transformed into a shared responsibility, each of us contributing based on our individual strengths and preferences. He handled the more structured tasks with his characteristic meticulousness, while I embraced the more creative endeavors, resulting in a home that reflected both our individual tastes and our collaborative efforts. The division of labor became a testament to our mutual respect, a demonstration that equality isn't about doing everything equally but about contributing equitably.

Our shared journey of discovery extended beyond our immediate circle. Our mutual respect became evident to our friends and family, who witnessed a transformation from strained interactions to genuine connections. His family, initially apprehensive about my unconventional nature, began to appreciate my unique contributions to his life, recognizing the love and respect that underpinned our evolving relationship. The bridges we'd built were not merely personal; they extended to our wider social circles, creating a more harmonious and supportive network of relationships.

One evening, as we sat together, reviewing photographs from our recent trip to a historic manor house, Benedict turned to me, a quiet smile playing on his lips. He didn't utter grand declarations of love; he didn't need to. The depth of his affection was palpable, evident in the gentle touch of his hand, the warmth in his gaze. The "taming," the initial premise of our relationship, had transmuted into something far more profound – a genuine partnership built on mutual respect, shared passions, and a deep appreciation for each other's inherent worth.

The journey had been transformative, not just for us individually, but for our relationship as a whole. The initial sparks of conflict had given way to a steady flame of mutual understanding, a testament to the power of empathy, compromise, and a willingness to embrace the messy, unpredictable beauty of love. The final chapter was still unwritten, but the story, with all its complexities and unexpected twists, was unfolding into a narrative far richer and more satisfying than any predetermined plot could have ever imagined. The "taming," in its unexpected way, had tamed us both, forging a partnership that celebrated individuality while cherishing the profound bond of mutual respect and shared affection. And that, I realized, was a love story worth writing.

REDEFINING TAMING

The rain lashed against the windows of our little cottage, mirroring the tempest brewing inside me – a tempest not of anger, but of introspection. Benedict, oblivious to my internal turmoil, was engrossed in meticulously arranging his spice rack, a task he approached with the same obsessive precision he applied to everything in his life. He hummed a jaunty tune, completely unaware of the revolution unfolding within me.

My initial mission, my self-appointed task of "taming" Benedict, had begun as a playful challenge, a cheeky subversion of the classic narrative. I'd envisioned myself as a modern-day Katherine, subtly shaping him, molding him into a more...adventurous, less rigidly structured version of himself. But the reality, as it so often does, had proved far more nuanced, far more complex than my initial, somewhat simplistic plan.

The culinary catastrophes, the pottery mishaps, the endless debates about literary interpretations – these weren't battles to be won, but shared experiences to be savored. Each misstep, each moment of friction, had served only to deepen our understanding, to chip away at the layers of preconceived notions we both held. I'd come to realize that "taming" wasn't about control; it was about mutual growth, a shared journey of self-discovery.

It wasn't about making him *become* someone else, but about helping him *discover* the person he already was, hidden beneath layers of routine and rigid self-imposed limitations. My initial approach had been, in retrospect, somewhat... colonialist. As if I could simply impose my worldview, my

preferences, my definition of "fun" onto him. The error of my ways was dawning on me with the relentless force of the storm outside.

Benedict, for all his rigid adherence to schedules and his almost neurotic need for order, possessed a surprising depth of compassion, a gentle kindness that had gradually revealed itself through the cracks in his meticulously constructed façade. His meticulous nature wasn't a flaw; it was a strength, a testament to his dedication, his unwavering commitment to those he cared for. It was simply...different from mine.

And that difference, I now realised, was not something to be eradicated, but something to be celebrated. The beauty of our relationship lay not in our similarities, but in the fascinating contrast between our personalities, the way our contrasting traits complemented each other, creating a dynamic equilibrium that was both intriguing and satisfying.

My own impulsive nature, often a source of frustration for him, was now seen as a counterpoint to his methodical approach, a source of spontaneity and adventure that prevented our lives from becoming too stagnant, too predictable. His methodical planning, in turn, provided a much-needed anchor to my often chaotic existence, preventing me from being swept away by my own unpredictable currents.

It was a delicate balance, this dance between order and chaos, a constant negotiation that required patience, understanding, and a willingness to compromise. There were still moments of friction, of course – we weren't suddenly perfect, perfectly synchronized beings. But these moments were now approached with a newfound maturity, a shared

understanding that allowed us to navigate them with grace and empathy.

Instead of launching into defensive arguments, we now took the time to understand each other's perspectives, to identify the root causes of the conflict, and to find mutually acceptable solutions. It wasn't about winning an argument; it was about finding common ground, about building a bridge of understanding instead of erecting walls of division.

This newfound maturity extended beyond our personal lives, permeating our professional collaborations as well. Our differing approaches, once a source of conflict, now became a source of strength, our complementary skills synergistically enhancing each other's contributions. His methodical approach ensured precision and accuracy, while my impulsive creativity provided the spark of innovation, the unexpected twist that often led to breakthrough moments.

The realization that "taming" wasn't about control, but about mutual respect and understanding, was a watershed moment in our relationship. It wasn't a sudden epiphany, but a gradual dawning, a slow and steady unfolding of truth, like a flower hesitantly opening its petals to the morning sun. It was a moment of profound selfawareness, a recognition of my own flaws and preconceived notions.

The journey hadn't been easy; there were still moments of doubt, of insecurity, of those familiar nagging anxieties that plague even the most secure of relationships. But these moments were now met with a newfound resilience, a shared determination to navigate the complexities of love and commitment with honesty, empathy, and an unwavering belief in the strength of our bond.

The storm outside had finally subsided, replaced by a soft, melancholic twilight. Benedict, having completed his spice rack organization with evident satisfaction, turned to me, a gentle smile gracing his lips. He didn't utter grand declarations of love; he didn't need to. His love was evident in his quiet presence, in the warmth of his gaze, in the gentle touch of his hand as he reached out to take mine.

It wasn't a fairy tale ending; it was a realistic, nuanced portrayal of a relationship evolving, growing, and deepening with each shared experience, each shared challenge, each shared laugh. The "taming," my initial, somewhat misguided project, had transformed into something far more profound – a partnership built on mutual respect, shared passions, and a deep appreciation for each other's unique and often contradictory qualities. And that, I realized, was a love story far more satisfying, far more real, than any predictable happily-ever-after. The rain had stopped, and a rainbow, faint but luminous, arched across the darkening sky. Our journey, like that rainbow, held the promise of countless more shades of wonder and unexpected beauty.

MOVING FORWARD

The scent of woodsmoke and brewing Earl Grey hung in the air, a comforting aroma that mirrored the quiet contentment settling over our little cottage. Benedict, ever the pragmatist, was already sketching out floor plans on a napkin, his brow furrowed in concentration. "Darling," he announced, without looking up, "I've been considering the feasibility of extending the conservatory."

I chuckled, leaning against the kitchen counter, a mug of steaming tea warming my hands. His dedication to practicality, once a source of frustration, now struck me as endearingly charming. "A conservatory? In this weather?" I teased, gesturing towards the persistent drizzle outside.

"One must think ahead," he replied, his voice laced with a hint of his usual dry humour. "And besides, a larger conservatory would provide ample space for your...creative pursuits." He glanced at the halffinished pottery project still sitting on the windowsill – a rather lopsided vase that bore a striking resemblance to a startled penguin.

My initial attempt to "tame" Benedict, to mold him into my idealized vision of a partner, had been a resounding failure – or perhaps, a spectacular success, depending on how you look at it. I had envisioned a whirlwind romance, a playful battle of wits, but what I'd found was something far more profound: a deep, abiding connection forged in the crucible of mutual understanding and respect.

The initial friction, the clashes of personality, had been replaced by a comfortable rhythm, a dance of compromise and collaboration. He'd learned to appreciate my impulsive

nature, my bursts of unexpected creativity, while I'd come to value his meticulous planning, his unwavering dedication, and his surprisingly gentle heart, hidden beneath layers of pragmatism. We were learning to celebrate our differences, to embrace the unique perspectives that each of us brought to the relationship.

The conservatory, I realized, was more than just an architectural project; it was a symbol of our future together. It represented our shared commitment to growth, to building something lasting and meaningful, a haven built on the foundations of mutual respect and shared dreams.

"I think," I said, thoughtfully swirling my tea, "that a conservatory would be lovely. But perhaps we should consider incorporating a small, wellventilated studio space within it?" My pottery experiments, however disastrous, had ignited a latent passion for ceramics.

Benedict, without missing a beat, adjusted his calculations on the napkin. "A studio? Excellent idea. We could incorporate ample natural light, perhaps a kiln... and definitely reinforced shelving for your... accumulating collection of clay." He looked at me with a smile that held a touch of amused understanding. He knew that my "collection" was more of a chaotic explosion of half-finished projects, and he didn't flinch.

Our conversations now flowed effortlessly, a seamless blend of practical planning and whimsical daydreaming. We discussed career goals – his ambition to publish his meticulously researched book on the history of spices, my desire to finally showcase my artistic talents in a local exhibition – and personal aspirations – weekend trips to explore hidden corners of the English countryside, learning to tango, adopting a rescue dog, maybe even learning to play

the ukulele (a prospect that filled Benedict with a quiet sense of dread, but one he was willing to tackle for me).

The initial "taming" had transformed into something altogether different: a collaborative project of self-discovery, a shared journey of growth and understanding. We were sculpting not just our home, but our lives together, shaping our future with careful precision and joyful abandon. And the beauty of it was that there was no single blueprint, no pre-ordained plan to follow. We were creating our own story, a unique narrative built on mutual respect, unwavering support, and a shared belief in the power of a love that transcended the simplistic expectations of a fairy-tale ending.

Later that evening, curled up on the sofa, Benedict reading aloud from a dusty volume of poetry while I sketched whimsical designs for our future conservatory, a profound sense of peace settled over me. The storm had passed, the tempest within had subsided. There were no more battles to be won, no more selves to tame. We were simply two individuals, imperfect yet perfectly suited, building a life together, one brick, one pot, one shared laugh at a time.

The "taming" had been a misguided metaphor from the start. It wasn't about subduing or controlling, but about embracing the complexities of a relationship, navigating the choppy waters of compromise and conflict with grace and understanding. It was about celebrating the unique blend of personalities, finding harmony in the contrasting rhythms of life. It was, in essence, a collaborative masterpiece, a work of art built not on dominance, but on mutual respect, shared dreams, and an unwavering commitment to nurturing the extraordinary bond that had blossomed between us.

Our journey together was not a straight line, a predictable path leading to a neatly packaged "happily ever after." It was a meandering road, filled with unexpected detours, scenic overlooks, and moments of breathtaking beauty. There were moments of frustration, of disagreement, of those inevitable conflicts that arise in any close relationship. But these moments, once sources of bitter conflict, were now approached with a newfound maturity, a shared understanding that allowed us to navigate them with grace and empathy. We learned to listen, not just to hear, to understand the nuances of each other's perspectives, and to find common ground even in the midst of disagreement.

We found solace in the simple rituals of our daily lives: the quiet moments shared over a cup of tea, the shared laughter echoing through the small cottage, the silent companionship during rainy evenings spent curled up on the sofa. These were the moments that nurtured our bond, the threads that wove the rich tapestry of our unique love story.

The future, as always, remained an unwritten page, a vast canvas waiting to be filled with the strokes of our shared experiences. But the foundation was secure, built on the bedrock of mutual respect, unwavering commitment, and the joyous understanding that true love isn't about taming, but about celebrating the unique and often contradictory beauty of two souls intertwined. The extension to the conservatory, like our relationship, was a work in progress, a dynamic and ever-evolving testament to the power of love, growth, and the enduring beauty of a partnership built on mutual respect and shared dreams. The rain outside had stopped, and a soft glow of twilight painted the sky. And as I watched Benedict's profile, illuminated by the soft lamplight, I knew, with absolute certainty, that our journey, like the endless horizon, held the promise of infinite wonder and limitless love.

The story wasn't finished; it was only just beginning.

NEW CHALLENGES
NEW PERSPECTIVES

The arrival of Benedict's eccentric Aunt Mildred, a woman whose wardrobe seemed to consist entirely of brightly coloured paisley and an unwavering belief in the healing power of crystals, presented our newly established domestic bliss with its first significant challenge. Mildred, a whirlwind of flamboyant energy and unsolicited advice, descended upon our cottage like a technicolour hurricane, bringing with her not only a mountain of luggage but also a healthy dose of chaos. She immediately declared the conservatory extension plans "utterly lacking in feng shui," insisted on rearranging the furniture according to the alignment of the planets, and attempted to introduce Benedict to the joys of competitive ferret legging (a sport I, frankly, found deeply disturbing).

Benedict, ever the pragmatist, initially attempted to navigate this onslaught of eccentricity with his usual calm and measured approach. He patiently explained the structural limitations of the conservatory extension, attempted to gently dissuade her from rearranging the furniture (a task that involved a rather tense standoff involving a particularly stubborn armchair and a rather determined Aunt Mildred), and politely declined her invitation to participate in ferret legging, citing a pre-existing engagement involving a rather important deadline for his spice history book. However, his patience began to fray at the edges as Mildred's interventions became increasingly intrusive. She insisted on preparing meals consisting entirely of kale and seaweed ("for the chakra alignment, darling"), redecorated the bathroom in a questionable shade of turquoise, and attempted to teach me the art of communicating with houseplants through telepathy.

My initial reaction was amusement. Aunt Mildred was a force of nature, a walking, talking contradiction that defied easy categorization. But as her eccentricities began to impinge on our routine, a subtle tension began to emerge between Benedict and me. He retreated into his work, his usual dry humour replaced by a quiet frustration. I, in turn, found myself caught between defending my partner and appeasing my increasingly disruptive relative. The carefully constructed equilibrium of our relationship seemed to teeter on the brink of collapse.

It was during a particularly chaotic evening, amidst a flurry of flying crystals, a near-miss with a rogue ferret, and a kale- based culinary disaster, that I realized the mistake we'd made. We'd been so focused on building our relationship, on nurturing our mutual understanding, that we hadn't adequately prepared for the inevitable external pressures that would test our resilience. We'd built a strong foundation, but we hadn't considered the potential for unforeseen storms.

The arrival of Aunt Mildred wasn't just a quirky inconvenience; it was a test, a crucible that would determine the true strength of our partnership.

The solution, as it often did, came unexpectedly. It wasn't a grand gesture, nor a dramatic confrontation; instead, it was a quiet conversation, a shared moment of vulnerability and understanding. We talked, not about Aunt Mildred's eccentricities, but about our feelings, our frustrations, and our fears. We acknowledged our individual weaknesses – Benedict's inability to set boundaries, my tendency to overthink and overcompensate – and began to strategize, to build a collaborative approach to managing the situation.

Benedict discovered a surprising strength, a newfound assertiveness. He learned to set firm, yet respectful, boundaries with his aunt, politely but firmly deflecting her

more outlandish suggestions. He even managed to negotiate a compromise on the conservatory's design, incorporating some of Mildred's feng shui principles while maintaining the structural integrity of the building. I, in turn, learned to temper my desire to please everyone, to prioritize our shared well-being over the need to avoid conflict. We worked together, supporting each other, learning to navigate the turbulent waters of family dynamics with a renewed sense of partnership and mutual support.

Aunt Mildred, surprisingly, proved to be a catalyst for growth. Her disruptive presence forced us to confront our weaknesses, to strengthen our communication, and to build a more resilient relationship. She left, eventually, leaving behind a trail of colourful paisley, a slightly rearranged kitchen, and a newfound appreciation for the importance of setting boundaries. But she also left behind something else: a deeper, more profound understanding of each other, a shared sense of accomplishment, and a stronger bond forged in the crucible of a shared challenge.

Our journey continued, taking unexpected turns and navigating new challenges. There were moments of doubt, moments of frustration, and moments when we questioned our ability to navigate the complexities of a modern relationship. But each challenge became a stepping stone, a lesson learned, a testament to our resilience. We learned to anticipate obstacles, to plan for unforeseen circumstances, and to approach conflict not as a battle to be won, but as an opportunity for growth and understanding.

We discovered the importance of shared hobbies, finding joy in quiet evenings spent painting pottery together (my skill still far exceeding Benedict's), attending local farmers' markets, and exploring hidden corners of the English countryside. We embraced the spontaneity of life, making

impulsive decisions that, in hindsight, always seemed to lead us to unexpected adventures. And, yes, we even attempted to learn the tango, a process that involved a considerable amount of laughter, a few near-misses with furniture, and a mutual agreement that we'd leave the professional tangoing to the experts.

Our lives weren't a fairy tale, devoid of conflict and hardship. But they were real, vibrant, and filled with a love that deepened with each challenge overcome. The "taming" metaphor, initially intended as a playful subversion of traditional gender roles, had evolved into something far more profound. It wasn't about control or conformity but about the mutual growth, the shared journey of two individuals learning, laughing, and loving their way through life's unpredictable paths. Our relationship was a work in progress, constantly evolving, a tapestry woven from the threads of laughter, compromise, and an unwavering commitment to each other.

The conservatory, finally completed, stood as

a testament to this journey. It was a haven of light and warmth, a sanctuary where we could retreat from the storms of life and find solace in each other's company. It was more than just a room; it was a symbol of our resilience, our growth, and our unwavering commitment to building a life together, brick by brick, laugh by laugh, and challenge by challenge. The future remained unwritten, a canvas waiting for our creative touch. And as we stood together, gazing at our completed project, bathed in the warm glow of the setting sun, I knew, with unwavering certainty, that our story, like life itself, was a beautiful, messy, and endlessly captivating journey.

CELEBRATING SUCCESSES

The scent of freshly baked bread, a triumphant aroma that battled valiantly against the lingering memory of Aunt Mildred's kale-andseaweed concoctions, filled our cottage. Benedict, his face flushed with a mixture of exertion and pride, carefully removed a golden-brown loaf from the oven. This wasn't just any loaf; it was the culmination of weeks of dedicated effort, a testament to his newfound passion for baking, a passion ignited ironically by Aunt Mildred's culinary disasters. He'd started with disastrous results – flat, dense loaves that bore a disconcerting resemblance to hockey pucks – but with each failed attempt, his determination had only grown stronger. He'd immersed himself in the art of baking, poring over ancient recipes, experimenting with different flours and techniques, until finally, success had arrived.

Holding the perfect loaf aloft, he grinned, a genuine, unadulterated smile that reached his eyes. "Behold," he announced with mock solemnity, "the masterpiece! A testament to patience, precision, and a healthy dose of stubbornness."

I laughed, the sound echoing through our cozy kitchen. "And a surprisingly delicious-smelling testament to overcoming culinary adversity," I added, reaching out to gently touch his arm. The past few weeks hadn't been without their challenges. The lingering effects of Aunt Mildred's visit had been a bit like the aftertaste of a particularly potent chilli; a lingering burn that required careful nurturing to soothe. But we'd navigated those turbulent waters, emerging stronger and more connected than ever. Benedict's baking journey became a metaphor for our own relationship, a journey

marked by setbacks and triumphs, where the lessons learned were as valuable as the final result.

We shared that loaf of bread, a simple act that symbolised the depth of our connection. With each bite, we toasted not just the bread, but our individual and shared victories. We celebrated his baking triumph, his newfound confidence in the kitchen. We acknowledged my own progress in finding a healthier balance between pleasing others and prioritizing my own needs. And we celebrated the strengthening bond between us, forged in the crucible of challenges faced and overcome.

Later that evening, nestled on the sofa with

a glass of wine, we reviewed our progress on individual projects. Benedict discussed the progress of his spice history book, his voice animated as he shared anecdotes from his research. He'd even managed to incorporate some of Aunt Mildred's (slightly misguided) theories on the metaphysical properties of spices – a touch of humour that made me laugh out loud. He'd found a way to weave her chaotic energy into his work, transforming a potential nuisance into a source of unique inspiration.

My own creative work hadn't been neglected either. I was finally putting the finishing touches on my novel, a witty, modern reimagining of a classic fairy tale, a project I'd secretly harboured for years. The characters, the plot twists, even the subtle social commentary – it all flowed effortlessly, a testament to the calm and inspired state of mind I'd cultivated since resolving the Mildred-induced chaos. The words seemed to write themselves, each sentence a testament to the newfound emotional equilibrium in my life. It was as if the resolution of the Aunt Mildred saga had unlocked a creative wellspring within me.

The conversation drifted to the future, to our shared dreams and ambitions. We talked about the possibility of travelling, perhaps exploring the spice markets of Morocco, a journey inspired by Benedict's research. We discussed potential collaborations, the exciting prospect of combining our creative talents in a joint project – perhaps a screenplay based on my novel. The future seemed limitless, a vibrant canvas waiting to be painted with our shared visions.

Evenings like these, filled with quiet intimacy, shared laughter, and the palpable sense of accomplishment, were precious. They were a reminder that our relationship wasn't just about romance, but about mutual support, shared growth, and the unwavering commitment to building a life together, one brick at a time. It wasn't about a perfect, fairytale existence; it was about the reality of navigating life's challenges, supporting each other, and cherishing the small victories along the way.

The following weeks saw us tackle new challenges with a newfound sense of collaborative teamwork. A sudden burst pipe, a neighbour's overly enthusiastic garden gnome collection, and even a rogue squirrel invasion – each presented a fresh opportunity to test our resilience, our communication skills, and our ability to handle life's little curveballs with grace, humour, and a healthy dose of teamwork.

We tackled the burst pipe with remarkable efficiency, a testament to our newfound ability to communicate effectively during moments of stress. Benedict, armed with his newfound problem-solving skills, managed to shut off the water supply and contact a plumber, while I ensured our home remained safe. We divided and conquered, each playing to our strengths and relying on the other for support.

The neighbour's gnome collection initially seemed an insurmountable obstacle – a veritable army of ceramic garden gnomes marching across their property. However, a simple, polite conversation yielded a surprising result. The neighbour, a rather eccentric woman named Agnes, confessed to her love for gnome collecting and her desire to share this passion with the world. Instead of conflict, we found a connection over shared love of unique hobbies.

Agnes invited us to join her Gnome Appreciation Society, a monthly gathering where everyone shares their love of gnomes and creates miniature gnome-sized landscapes. It felt like a bizarre, yet oddly delightful twist of fate.

The squirrel invasion required a different tactic. Benedict, using his knowledge of animal behaviour and a generous supply of peanuts, successfully persuaded the squirrels to relocate to a nearby park, leaving behind only a scattering of nutshells as a reminder of their brief occupation. It was a testament to his patience and creative problemsolving abilities.

These challenges, though seemingly trivial, proved to be valuable lessons in our ongoing journey. They solidified our partnership, deepening our trust and strengthening our bond. They showed us that a relationship, like a perfectly baked loaf of bread, is not merely about the final result, but about the process of working together, overcoming obstacles, and celebrating both the big and the small victories along the way. The "taming" metaphor had long since lost its initial playful edge, replaced by a deeper understanding of mutual respect, shared growth, and a love that was as complex, unpredictable, and ultimately rewarding as life itself. Our relationship was a testament to the power of collaboration, resilience, and a shared commitment to building a life that was not just comfortable and predictable, but also exciting, challenging, and deeply fulfilling.

We were not just a couple; we were a team, a partnership forged in the fires of adversity, strengthened by shared laughter and mutual support. Our story was a testament to the beautiful messiness of life, the unexpected detours, the unforeseen challenges, and the enduring power of love to guide us through the unpredictable landscapes of a modern relationship. The future remained uncertain, but with each challenge overcome, we felt better equipped, more confident, and more deeply in love than ever before. And that, I realised, was the greatest success of all.

LEARNING FROM THE PAST

The fire crackled merrily in the hearth, casting dancing shadows across the walls of our cottage. Outside, the wind howled a mournful ballad, a stark contrast to the warmth and contentment within. We sat nestled on the sofa, a half- finished bottle of wine between us, the remnants of a particularly delicious cheese and chutney board scattered on the coffee table. Silence, comfortable and companionable, settled between us, a silence punctuated only by the occasional sigh of contentment or the crackling of the fire.

"Remember Aunt Mildred's... advice on courtship?" Benedict chuckled, a low rumble in his chest. His voice held a mixture of amusement and a hint of something akin to wistful fondness. He swirled the remaining wine in his glass, the amber liquid catching the firelight.

I smiled, the memory bringing a wave of both amusement and a touch of lingering incredulity. Aunt Mildred's "advice," delivered with the force of a hurricane and the questionable accuracy of a particularly unreliable horoscope, had certainly been... memorable. Her pronouncements on the delicate art of "taming" a man had bordered on the absurd, a blend of outdated social norms and frankly bizarre interpretations of ancient texts. She'd suggested everything from reciting Shakespeare to mastering the art of silent, steely-eyed stares, all in the name of achieving marital bliss, or at least, what she perceived as marital bliss.

"Let's just say her methods were... unconventional," I replied, choosing my words carefully. Unconventional was a polite euphemism. Explosive, unorthodox, downright bonkers – those terms came closer to capturing the essence

of her approach. Yet, looking back, I had to admit a grudging respect for her unwavering commitment to her own (albeit misguided) convictions.

"And yet," Benedict added, his eyes twinkling, "her pronouncements, however bizarre, sparked a fascinating conversation – a conversation that ultimately led us to a far deeper understanding of ourselves and our relationship."

He was right. Aunt Mildred's visit, while initially chaotic, had inadvertently forced us to confront some long-standing assumptions and insecurities. It had brought to the surface some unresolved issues, prompting us to engage in honest, sometimes uncomfortable, conversations about our expectations, our needs, and our hopes for the future. In a strange, ironic twist, her attempts to manipulate our relationship had inadvertently strengthened it.

"It was like a pressure cooker," I mused, swirling the remaining wine in my glass. "All that pent-up tension, those unspoken anxieties – she released it all, leaving us with the difficult task of cleaning up the mess, but also the opportunity to rebuild our relationship on a much stronger foundation."

We discussed the specific incidents that had stood out, the moments where Aunt Mildred's interference had triggered a deeper understanding. Benedict recounted how her attempts to control his schedule had led him to confront his own anxieties about work-life balance, prompting him to reassess his priorities and rediscover the joy in his writing. He had started to prioritize his own creative endeavors, setting aside dedicated time for research and writing, a practice he'd often neglected in the past.

I, in turn, admitted how her criticisms of my independence had encouraged me to reflect on my own tendencies to strive for perfection. I had always pushed myself relentlessly, striving to meet everyone's expectations while neglecting my own needs and desires. Aunt

Mildred's interference had made it all the clearer that I needed to establish more healthy boundaries. I had started to learn the fine art of saying "no" without guilt, a skill that had proved surprisingly liberating. This wasn't a matter of being "tamed," but of becoming more authentically myself.

Our conversation drifted to the lessons we'd learned about communication. We had always communicated well, or so we thought. But Aunt Mildred's interference had revealed some subtle communication breakdowns, some unspoken assumptions that had been simmering beneath the surface. We had learned the importance of actively listening, of expressing our needs clearly and respectfully, and of finding ways to navigate disagreements without resorting to conflict.

The incident with the rogue squirrel invasion was a perfect example. While initially amusing, it had forced us to work together, to solve problems creatively, and to appreciate each other's strengths. Benedict's patience and understanding of animal behaviour had been invaluable, while my ability to remain calm and offer support had balanced his approach.

The gnome incident, another seeming absurdity, had encouraged us to open ourselves to different perspectives and forge unlikely friendships.

We realised that our relationship wasn't about

dominance or control; it was about mutual respect, shared growth, and a willingness to learn from each other. The concept of "taming," once a playful metaphor, had been thoroughly dismantled and replaced with a far richer, more complex, and ultimately more satisfying understanding of partnership.

It

was not about molding each other into predetermined roles, but about celebrating our differences and supporting each other's individual growth.

The fire crackled, and the wind howled softly outside. But within our cozy cottage, there was warmth, contentment, and a profound sense of shared accomplishment. We had navigated the turbulent waters of Aunt Mildred's visit, emerging stronger, wiser, and more deeply in love than before. Our journey had been far from conventional, but it had been ours, a unique testament to the beautiful complexity of modern love. It was a testament to the power of resilience, shared laughter, and a willingness to learn from the past, even from the most unconventional of teachers. The past few weeks had been a crucible, forging a bond that was as strong, as enduring, and as richly textured as the perfectly baked loaf of bread we'd shared just weeks earlier. That bread, a symbol of Benedict's journey of self-discovery, represented a larger truth about our relationship: growth, collaboration and the sweetness of unexpected achievements. The future remained unwritten, an exciting, perhaps slightly chaotic, canvas awaiting our collaborative masterpiece. And, we realised, with a shared smile, we were perfectly ready to tackle it, together.

LOOKING AHEAD

The morning sun streamed through the kitchen window, painting stripes of gold across the worn wooden floorboards. Benedict, humming a jaunty tune, was already at work, his hands expertly kneading dough, the rhythmic motion a counterpoint to the cheerful chirping of birds outside. The air hummed with a quiet contentment, a stark contrast to the tempestuous weeks that had preceded. Aunt Mildred's visit, once a source of considerable stress, now felt like a distant, slightly surreal dream, a bizarre interlude in an otherwise harmonious narrative.

I watched him, a mug of steaming tea warming my hands. The transformation in Benedict had been remarkable. He was no longer the perpetually stressed, slightly harried man I had known. He was more relaxed, more present, more... himself. The pressure cooker, as I'd termed it, had undeniably exerted its pressure, but the resulting steam had cleared the air, leaving behind a space for genuine growth and understanding.

He looked up, catching my gaze, and smiled,

a genuine, heart-warming smile that reached his eyes. "Good morning, my love," he said, his voice soft and full of affection. "The bread is coming along nicely. I think today's loaf might even surpass the last one."

The bread, a symbol of his newfound creative confidence, had become a recurring motif in our evolving narrative. Each loaf he baked represented a step forward, a testament to his ability to manage his time, nurture his talent, and prioritize his own well-being. The initial loaves had been a bit... experimental. A touch too dense, a little underbaked, a

testament to his still-developing skills. But each subsequent loaf was an improvement, a reflection of his growing mastery of his craft, mirroring his overall personal growth.

"I wouldn't doubt it," I replied, my voice mirroring his gentle tone. "You seem to have found your rhythm, both in the kitchen and... everywhere else."

We fell into a comfortable silence, the only sound the gentle hiss of the kettle and the rhythmic thud of Benedict's hands working the dough. It was a silence filled with unspoken understanding, a testament to the growth we had both experienced. The conversation, our shared journey, had broadened our understanding of each other and ourselves. It had uncovered previously unknown facets of our personalities and our approach to life.

Later that day, we strolled hand-in-hand through the nearby park, the autumn leaves crunching beneath our feet. The air was crisp and clean, the sky a vast, breathtaking canvas of cerulean blue. We spoke little, but the comfortable silence felt significant, filled with the shared understanding that words were sometimes unnecessary. The park, a familiar backdrop to our lives, felt different somehow, imbued with a newfound sense of peace and tranquility.

We stopped by a babbling brook, its water cascading over smooth, moss-covered stones. Benedict, ever the romantic, picked up a smooth, grey stone, perfectly shaped and polished by time and water.

"For you," he said, presenting it to me with a mischievous glint in his eye. "A memento of our... unconventional journey. A reminder of the unexpected beauty we've found along the way."

I smiled, taking the stone from his hand. It was cool and smooth to the touch, a perfect miniature representation of the enduring strength and resilience of our relationship. It was a reminder of how the most unlikely circumstances can forge the deepest bonds. Aunt Mildred's disastrous interference, once a source of immense frustration, had ironically served as a catalyst for positive change. It had forced us to confront our own vulnerabilities, our hidden anxieties, and the subtle ways we'd been neglecting our own needs.

The journey had certainly not been straightforward. There had been moments of frustration, of doubt, even of anger. The squirrel invasion, the gnome incident, Aunt Mildred's questionable advice – these were just a few of the unexpected hurdles we had overcome. Yet, each challenge had served to strengthen our bond, pushing us to communicate more honestly, to support each other unconditionally, and to appreciate each other's unique strengths.

That evening, we sat by the fire, the flames dancing and flickering, mirroring the warmth and joy in our hearts. We shared a quiet dinner, savouring the flavors of the meal, the quiet companionship as comforting as the crackling fire. It wasn't just the food that was delicious; it was the contentment, the sense of peace, and the unspoken awareness of our shared journey that made the moment special.

As the hours passed, we talked about the future, about our dreams, our ambitions, our hopes for the years ahead. We spoke of travel, of perhaps adopting a dog (after careful consideration, of course, and thorough research on the potential for future squirrel conflicts), of potentially expanding our home, or perhaps embarking on a new adventure, a long-delayed writing project that Benedict had been longing to pursue. The possibilities stretched before us, exciting and open-ended. It felt as if we were standing at the precipice of something extraordinary.

But beneath the excitement lay a profound sense of calm. We had weathered the storm; we had emerged stronger, wiser, and more deeply in love. We had learned to navigate conflict, to communicate honestly, and to appreciate each other's individuality. We had discovered that 'taming' was not about control or manipulation, but about mutual respect, growth, and a shared commitment to building a life together, on our own terms.

We weren't just a couple; we were a team, partners in life's grand adventure. We had discovered that true connection, true love, is not about molding each other into predetermined roles but about celebrating the unique, individual tapestry that together forms a rich and vibrant whole. The future stretched before us, an unwritten story awaiting our collaborative creation. And we were both ready to write it, together, pen in hand, ready to tackle whatever came our way, with laughter, love, and a healthy dose of shared amusement.

The past had been a catalyst, a crucible that had forged a bond stronger than we could ever have imagined. We were no longer just navigating Aunt Mildred's antiquated advice;

we were charting our own course, a path guided by mutual respect, shared goals, and a deep appreciation for the unexpected joys and challenges that life throws our way. We knew the path ahead wouldn't be easy; that life would inevitably throw new challenges our way. But we also knew, with absolute certainty, that we were ready for whatever came. We were a team, partners in the truest sense, ready to face the future, together, one perfectly baked loaf of bread at a time. And that, more than anything, was a truly comforting

thought. The future, whatever it held, was ours to shape, to share, to enjoy, together. And that, we both knew, was a truly magnificent beginning.

INTRODUCING KATHERINES CIRCLE

The following weekend, Benedict and I hosted a small gathering. It wasn't a grand affair, just a relaxed get-together at our home, a casual affair designed to introduce Benedict to my closest friends and family. I'd anticipated some raised eyebrows, perhaps a few pointed questions, maybe even a subtle sniff of disapproval from certain quarters. After all, our relationship, even after the successful navigation of Aunt Mildred's interference, was still relatively new, and our unconventional path to understanding had hardly been conventional. My friends, however, were a fairly tolerant bunch, a motley crew united by a shared sense of humour and a lack of concern for societal norms.

First to arrive was Esme, my oldest friend, a whirlwind of energy and sharp wit. She surveyed Benedict with a knowing smirk, her eyes twinkling with amusement. "So," she announced, leaning in conspiratorially, "the bread-making artiste. Is this the secret to your newfound domestic bliss?" Her tone was teasing, but her affection was undeniable.

Benedict, ever the charmer, chuckled. "The bread is merely a byproduct of a more significant transformation, Esme. A journey of selfdiscovery, if you will." He winked, his confidence a refreshing contrast to the hesitant man I'd initially introduced to my circle. Esme's laughter filled the room, echoing my own relief. The man before me was clearly comfortable in his own skin, and that, more than anything, made my heart swell.

Next came Clara, my cousin, a staunch traditionalist who usually brought a dose of slightly judgmental scrutiny to any social gathering.
She observed Benedict with a measured

gaze, her lips pressed into a thin line. She'd always been a stickler for decorum, a woman who believed in societal norms and expectations. I braced myself for the inevitable.

"He seems... different," Clara commented, her tone betraying a hint of uncertainty. "Much more... relaxed." She paused, seemingly searching for the right words. "Not quite the stressed-out workaholic you described last time, then."

I suppressed a smile. Clara's surprise was a testament to Benedict's transformation. The man who'd once resembled a tightly wound spring was now relaxed, confident, even playful. He'd embraced his creative side, found a balance in his life, and even tackled his infamous squirrel phobia. I had a feeling Clara was secretly impressed, even if she wouldn't admit it.

Then there was Leo, my brother, a cynical journalist with a penchant for dissecting human relationships with the same ruthless efficiency he applied to political scandals. He greeted Benedict with a curt nod, his usual skepticism palpable. "So," he began, his voice laced with dry irony, "the great taming has begun, has it? Or perhaps it's more of a mutual... refinement process?" He raised an eyebrow, his gaze pointedly fixed on Benedict.

Benedict met his gaze head-on, his expression calm and self- assured. "Mutual growth, Leo. I prefer the term 'mutual growth' to 'taming'," he said, his tone both polite and assertive. The response was unexpected, even to me, but he handled the situation with a self-assured composure that surprised even me.

The evening progressed with a mixture of lively conversation, gentle teasing, and surprisingly warm interactions. My friends and family, initially hesitant and

guarded, gradually relaxed, charmed by Benedict's quiet charm, intelligence, and surprisingly good sense of humour. They discovered a depth to his character that had initially been masked by his stress and anxieties. They started to see him not as an object of my 'taming' but as an individual with his own unique strengths and vulnerabilities.

Later, as the guests were departing, Esme pulled me aside, her voice hushed. "He's... actually quite delightful," she confessed, a genuine smile lighting up her face. "You've done well, Katherine. I admit, I had my reservations."

Clara, ever the pragmatic one, nodded in agreement. "I still believe some of his habits need addressing, particularly his overuse of the phrase "holistic approach" but overall," she conceded, "he's much improved. I am particularly impressed by his mastery of the sourdough starter."

Even Leo offered a begrudging compliment. "He's... tolerable," he admitted, a rare flash of something resembling amusement in his eyes. "And surprisingly adept at deflecting my more pointed questions."

The reactions of my friends and family were a clear indication of how much Benedict had changed. It wasn't merely a matter of external adjustments; it was a transformation that ran deeper, a fundamental shift in his mindset, his approach to life, his very being. The initial skepticism had been replaced by genuine acceptance, a testament to his profound personal growth and, perhaps, to my ability to navigate a relationship that challenged conventional expectations.

The evening ended with a sense of contented warmth. The initial apprehension had dissipated, replaced by a feeling of quiet satisfaction.

I'd introduced Benedict to my circle, not

with the aim of seeking approval or validation, but rather to share a significant part of my life, a part that had enriched me beyond measure. The responses I received were a validation, not of his adherence to societal norms, but of the genuine connection we had forged, a connection strong enough to overcome expectations and prejudices.

The next few weeks passed in a flurry of activity, a peaceful rhythm that contrasted sharply with the chaotic period that had preceded it. Benedict continued his baking experiments, each loaf a masterpiece, a reflection of his growing confidence and self-assurance. He started taking evening classes in pottery, his hands now as comfortable shaping clay as they were kneading dough, his creative impulses finding new outlets, a testament to his growing belief in his own abilities. He'd also started running again, a far cry from the sedentary lifestyle he had once embraced, a symbol of his commitment to a healthier and more balanced approach to life.

One particularly crisp autumn afternoon, as we were strolling through the park, I noticed a profound shift in his personality. He was no longer the anxious, uncertain man I'd met. He was relaxed, confident, and radiating a quiet sense of self-assuredness. It wasn't just a transformation; it was a revelation. He was coming into his own, shedding the layers of self-doubt that had once held him captive, blossoming into the person he was always meant to be. He had discovered his own inner strength, a resilience that had been hidden beneath the layers of self-imposed pressure.

As the sun set, painting the sky in hues of fiery orange and deep violet, we sat on a park bench, hand in hand, the quiet contentment between us more profound than any grand gesture could ever express. We had weathered the storm, navigated the challenges, and emerged stronger, wiser, and

more deeply in love. Our journey had been unconventional, unexpected, even comical at times, but it had been ours, a testament to the resilience of the human spirit, to the transformative power of love, and to the enduring magic of a perfectly baked loaf of bread, a seemingly insignificant object which had somehow become a potent symbol of our shared growth and newfound happiness. The future, whatever it held, was ours to shape, to share, to enjoy, together. And that, we both knew, was a truly magnificent beginning.

BENEDICTS FAMILY DYNAMICS

The following weekend, I decided to introduce Benedict to my own family. This was a rather more daunting prospect than introducing him to my friends. My friends were, by and large, eccentrics who embraced the unconventional; my family, however, were... well, let's just say they were more rooted in tradition. My mother, bless her cotton socks, possessed an unwavering belief in the sanctity of cucumber sandwiches and the importance of matching china. My father, a retired solicitor with a penchant for Latin phrases and even stronger opinions, held a similar view of social decorum. And then there was my younger sister, Penelope, a whirlwind of chaotic energy and questionable fashion choices, who viewed the world through the lens of a particularly cynical romantic comedy. The potential for disaster was, to put it mildly, significant.

I'd spent the preceding week painstakingly prepping Benedict. We'd rehearsed polite conversation starters, reviewed appropriate table manners (apparently, Benedict had a habit of using his bread roll as a utensil during particularly heated debates, a habit I'd gently, yet firmly, discouraged), and even practiced a few subtle nods of agreement to my mother's more esoteric pronouncements on the merits of floral arrangements. He'd approached the task with surprising enthusiasm, a far cry from the initial resistance he'd shown to my attempts at, ahem, 'refinement.' This time, he seemed genuinely invested in making a good impression on my rather formidable family.

The family dinner was held, naturally, at my parents' house. It was a rather grand affair, a far cry from the relaxed gatherings I was accustomed to with my friends. The dining room, a testament to my mother's impeccable taste, was set with silverware that could have doubled as medieval weaponry, crystal glasses that shimmered like captured stars, and linen napkins that probably cost more than my weekly grocery bill. The air hummed with an unspoken tension, a subtle undercurrent of expectation that hung heavy in the room.

My mother, resplendent in a silk dress that resembled a particularly flamboyant garden, greeted Benedict with a smile that didn't quite reach her eyes. She'd already interrogated me relentlessly about his background, his job, his hobbies, and his – God forbid – his lineage. Benedict, however, remained unfazed. He greeted her with a charming smile and a polite inquiry about her latest floral arrangements, a masterstroke of diplomacy if I ever saw one.

My father, perched at the head of the table like a hawk surveying its prey, eyed Benedict with an expression that combined skepticism and thinly veiled suspicion. He peppered him with questions about his professional life, his political views, and even his preferred method of brewing tea (a surprisingly contentious topic within my family).

Benedict answered each question with calm grace and measured responses, his confidence a reassuring counterpoint to my mounting anxiety.

Penelope, seated opposite Benedict, adopted a silent observing role that belied her actual approach. Her eyes, however, were twinkling with amusement, hinting at the sarcastic commentary she'd likely be unleashing later. She even subtly kicked me under the table once in approval of his ability to deflect my father's barbed comments about 'modern artistic sensibilities'.

The conversation meandered through a series of seemingly harmless topics – the weather, the neighbours' noisy dog, the merits of various investment strategies – yet beneath the surface currents of polite conversation, a subtle clash of cultures played out. My family, firmly entrenched in their traditional world, looked upon Benedict's unconventional life choices with a mixture of bewilderment and disapproval, while Benedict, in turn, observed their rigid adherence to social norms with a gentle bemusement that masked a keen understanding of their underlying insecurities.

My father, in a particularly memorable moment, launched into a lengthy discourse on the importance of upholding tradition, illustrating his point with several questionable Latin proverbs and a rather dubious anecdote about his college days. Benedict, instead of engaging in a direct confrontation, listened intently, offering thoughtful comments that subtly countered my father's more rigid viewpoints. It was a dance of intellectual sparring, a delicate balance of respect and gentle disagreement, a fascinating display of social maneuvering that left me both impressed and amused.

The evening's highlight, or perhaps lowlight, depending on your perspective, involved Penelope's sudden decision to recount a rather embarrassing story about my father's youthful indiscretions – a tale involving a rather unfortunate incident with a flock of geese and a pair of ill-fitting trousers. The room erupted in a mixture of shocked silence and suppressed laughter. Even my father cracked a smile, though I suspect it was more a result of mortification than amusement. Benedict navigated this unexpected turn of events with remarkable composure, diverting the conversation towards a
discussion of the surprising culinary

versatility of geese, a tactful manoeuvre that spared my

father further embarrassment and ensured a smoother transition away from the potentially explosive topic.

Throughout the meal, Benedict skillfully navigated the complexities of my family's dynamics, deftly sidestepping potentially hazardous topics, answering difficult questions with a blend of wit and diplomacy, and even managing to elicit a few genuine smiles from my usually stoic mother. It wasn't just his charm or his ability to handle my father's verbal jousts that impressed my family. It was his genuine kindness, his respect for their opinions, even when he disagreed, and his ability to find common ground despite differing backgrounds.

By the end of the evening, the initial tension had visibly eased. My mother, rather surprisingly, complimented his choice of wine. My father, though he still harboured some reservations, conceded that Benedict was "not entirely unredeemable." Even Penelope, the queen of sarcastic commentary, offered a grudging nod of approval. The success of the evening wasn't a matter of Benedict conforming to my family's expectations, but rather his ability to connect with them on a human level, to forge relationships despite their cultural differences.

As Benedict and I departed, my mother even slipped me a whispered compliment: "He's... different," she conceded, her voice laced with a hint of wonder. "But not unpleasant, darling. Not unpleasant at all." This was high praise, indeed, coming from a woman who considered a misplaced napkin a major social faux pas.

The encounter with my family served as a powerful reminder that relationships are not about conforming to pre-defined moulds or adhering to rigid societal expectations. They're about embracing diversity, respecting differences, and

finding common ground amidst diverging worlds. Benedict's success in navigating my family's world was not about him changing, but about my family opening themselves to a different perspective, to a different way of being. And that, I realised, was perhaps the most significant achievement of all. It was a testament to the power of understanding, the strength of connection, and the enduring magic of a perfectly baked loaf of bread – a loaf that had, unexpectedly, become the symbol of a family bridging the gaps between their different worlds. The future, I realised, held a lot more of these kinds of trials. But with Benedict by my side, I knew, somehow, that we would face them together, armed with patience, humour, and a shared appreciation for perfectly risen dough.

BRIDGING THE GAP

The following week was dedicated to Operation: Family Harmony 2.0 – the friends' edition. This proved to be a significantly less formal, yet equally challenging, endeavour. My friends, a delightfully eclectic bunch, weren't known for their adherence to social graces or, for that matter, conventional behaviour. Introducing Benedict to this chaotic constellation of personalities was akin to releasing a carefully orchestrated symphony into a mosh pit.

First up was Esme, a performance artist with a penchant for dramatic entrances and even more dramatic exits. Her apartment, a kaleidoscope of vibrant colours and unsettling sculptures, immediately set the tone. Benedict, ever the diplomat, greeted her with a genuine enthusiasm that somehow managed to overshadow the slightly unnerving taxidermied squirrel perched precariously on her bookshelf. Esme, initially suspicious of anyone who didn't possess at least three visible tattoos and an opinion on the socio- political implications of glitter, surprisingly warmed to Benedict's calm demeanor and his ability to engage in a surprisingly insightful discussion on the existential angst of the modern mime.

Next came Leo, a writer perpetually battling writer's block and an even more persistent caffeine addiction. He greeted Benedict with a weary skepticism, questioning his very existence with a barrage of philosophical queries that would have stumped Socrates. Benedict, however, rose to the challenge, engaging in a witty exchange that cleverly skirted the potentially thorny issue of artistic merit while simultaneously managing to secure a recommendation for Leo's favourite brand of ethically-sourced coffee beans.

The grand finale was a gathering at Barnaby's, a self- proclaimed "eclectic emporium" that doubled as a bar, a gallery, and a haven for lost souls (and stray cats). Barnaby himself, a man whose personality could best be described as a chaotic explosion of colourful scarves and questionable life choices, introduced Benedict to a crowd that included a competitive yo-yo champion, a woman who claimed to be able to communicate with squirrels (the taxidermied one from Esme's apartment would likely disagree), and a man who was convinced he was a reincarnation of Leonardo da Vinci. Benedict navigated this surreal landscape with remarkable grace, effortlessly blending into the quirky tapestry of personalities, engaging in conversations about everything from the finer points of Renaissance art to the aerodynamic properties of a well-thrown yo-yo.

While my family's challenge was one of navigating traditional expectations, my friends' presented a different, equally complex set of hurdles – a battle against the unpredictable and the unconventional. It wasn't about adhering to a specific set of rules, but about adapting to the ever-shifting currents of their unique personalities. It was a testament to Benedict's adaptability, his ability to find common ground in the most unexpected places. He didn't try to change them; he simply accepted them, their quirks and idiosyncrasies, their chaotic energy and their unconventional perspectives. He listened, he laughed, he even attempted to learn a few yo-yo tricks.

The most surprising aspect of these interactions was the unexpected connection that formed between Benedict and my friends. They saw past his initial reserve, his seemingly 'ordinary' exterior, recognizing the depth and wit beneath the surface. They appreciated his genuine interest in their lives, his ability to listen without judgment, his willingness

to embrace the absurdity of their world. And perhaps most importantly, they saw in him a reflection of themselves – a shared appreciation for the unconventional, a similar fascination with the unique, the different.

These gatherings weren't simply introductions; they were a testament to the power of shared humanity, a demonstration of how seemingly disparate worlds could collide and connect, forging bonds of friendship amidst the chaos. It was a reminder that true connection transcends societal norms and expectations, that it thrives on embracing diversity, celebrating individuality, and finding common ground amidst the most unlikely of circumstances.

It was, in a way, a mirror image of Benedict's interactions with my family. With my family, it had been a process of gently nudging them towards a broader perspective, of expanding their understanding of different approaches to life. With my friends, it was about embracing their already expansive perspectives, recognizing the inherent value in their unorthodox ways of being. In both cases, the common thread was respect, understanding, and a shared appreciation for the richness of human experience, in all its messy, unconventional glory.

The differences between my family and friends extended beyond their approaches to life. My family represented a world of structured routines, of established hierarchies, of unspoken rules and expectations. My friends, on the other hand, inhabited a world of creative chaos, of spontaneous adventures, of ever-shifting alliances and loyalties. The challenge, I realised, lay not in reconciling these two seemingly disparate worlds, but in celebrating their unique qualities, in finding beauty in their contrasts, and in appreciating the diversity of human experience.

Benedict's success lay not in his ability to conform, but in his ability to connect, to bridge the gap between these different worlds, not by compromising his own identity, but by respectfully engaging with others' viewpoints. He embraced the challenges presented by both my family and friends, not as threats to his own sense of self, but as opportunities for growth, for connection, for a deeper understanding of himself and the world around him. He didn't try to 'tame' either group; he simply accepted them, flaws and all, celebrating the uniqueness that made them so wonderfully, and frustratingly, themselves.

The experience underscored a vital truth: relationships aren't about molding others to fit pre-conceived notions or expectations. They're about accepting differences, about celebrating individuality, about forging connections despite – or perhaps because of – the contrasts that define us.

Benedict's journey, my journey, wasn't about taming each other, but about growing together, about learning to navigate the complexities of our own selves and the people we chose to share our lives with. It was a journey of mutual respect, of shared laughter, and, unexpectedly, a newfound appreciation for the perfectly-brewed cup of ethicallysourced coffee. The journey of taming had transformed into a journey of understanding – and that, I realised, was far more rewarding. And dare I say, more fun.

The culmination of all these social acrobatics was a rather surreal joint birthday party for me and Penelope. We'd combined our celebrations in an attempt to streamline the social calendar and prevent any further catastrophic events. My family and my friends were invited, a risky gamble considering their dramatically different approaches to social interaction. Benedict, ever the peacemaker, was charged with the crucial role of social lubricant, a task he approached with his usual mix of quiet confidence and subtle wit.

The result was surprisingly harmonious, a testament to Benedict's diplomatic skills and perhaps a testament to the shared love of cake. The evening unfolded as a fascinating cultural exchange. My mother, ever the traditionalist, engaged in a surprisingly lively debate with Leo on the merits of vintage wine versus artisanal coffee, a debate that ended with an unexpected truce, sealed by a shared appreciation for the delicate balance of acidity and tannins. My father, initially skeptical of the bohemian crowd, found himself engaged in a surprisingly intellectual conversation with Esme about the existential angst of squirrels. Penelope, ever the cynic, even offered a grudging compliment to Barnaby's questionable fashion choices. And through it all, Benedict moved smoothly, navigating the currents of different personalities and perspectives, gently bridging the divides, creating a space where both worlds could coexist.

The evening wasn't just a successful social gathering, it was a microcosm of the larger narrative that had unfolded throughout our 'taming' adventure. It was a demonstration of the power of connection, of the strength that comes from embracing differences, of the potential for understanding to blossom even in the most unexpected circumstances. And, perhaps most importantly, it was a reaffirmation of the simple truth that relationships, whether familial or friendly, are not about control or conformity, but about respect, acceptance, and a willingness to embrace the complexities of human connection. The 'taming' experiment, it turned out, had evolved into something far more profound – a journey of mutual understanding, a celebration of diversity, and a testament to the enduring power of human connection. And, yes, of perfectly risen bread and ethically-sourced coffee.

The future, it seemed, wouldn't be about taming, but about navigating the delightful, and often chaotic, landscape of life, together.

NAVIGATING SOCIAL OBSTACLES

The aftermath of the joint birthday party left me feeling strangely... exhilarated. Exhausted, yes, but exhilarated. It was as if we'd successfully navigated a particularly treacherous rapids, emerging slightly damp but undeniably triumphant. Benedict, bless his pragmatic soul, had already started compiling a spreadsheet analyzing the success rates of various conversational strategies employed throughout the evening. I suspected it involved a complex algorithm factoring in variables like alcohol consumption, proximity to taxidermied squirrels, and the frequency of mentions of ethically sourced coffee.

His dedication to quantifying the social dynamics of a family-friends fusion party was, as always, both endearing and slightly terrifying. It spoke volumes about his methodical approach to life, a stark contrast to the beautifully chaotic lives of my friends and the rigidly structured existence of my family. He was, in essence, a bridge –

a perfectly calibrated, slightly quirky, and incredibly effective bridge connecting two wildly different worlds.

The following weeks were a quieter affair, a gentle ebb after the social tsunami of the birthday bash. This allowed us to consolidate our gains, to reflect on the lessons learned – and there were many. Benedict, for instance, had discovered a hidden talent for competitive yo-yoing, much to the amusement of Leo and the profound disapproval of my mother, who considered it a frivolous waste of time that could have been better spent on something... productive, like cross-stitching a portrait of the Queen.

My father, surprisingly, had developed a nascent interest in modern performance art, mostly driven by Esme's surprisingly persuasive arguments about the symbolic use of glitter. He even attempted to recreate one of her more abstract sculptures using garden gnomes and old coat hangers. The result was...unconventional, to say the least, but undeniably endearing.

Penelope, having witnessed the social alchemy of the birthday party, had mellowed slightly. Her cynicism, while still present, was now laced with a hint of grudging admiration. She even confessed to occasionally appreciating Barnaby's questionable fashion choices, a sentiment she swore she'd never utter aloud.

The social integration wasn't without its bumps. There were still moments of awkward silence, of clashing personalities, of unexpected philosophical debates erupting in the middle of a perfectly good cheese and wine pairing. But these were smaller, less dramatic skirmishes. The larger battles had been won, the major social obstacles navigated with surprising grace and a fair amount of comedic relief.

One particularly memorable incident involved a heated discussion between my mother and Leo about the merits of organic vegetables versus the efficiency of hydroponics. It was a clash of generations, a collision of ideologies, a debate that could have escalated into a fullblown family feud. But Benedict, with the diplomatic skills of a seasoned UN negotiator, intervened. He didn't attempt to mediate; he simply offered to grow both organic and hydroponic tomatoes in his surprisingly spacious balcony garden. He then presented the results – a side-by-side taste test, comparing the flavours and textures. The ensuing discussion became a fascinating exploration of agricultural techniques, devoid of the initial acrimony.

Another challenge came in the form of an unexpected visit from my Aunt Mildred, a woman whose social graces were as outdated as her wardrobe. Aunt Mildred, a self-proclaimed expert on etiquette and propriety, found Benedict's casual demeanor and my friends' bohemian lifestyle utterly appalling. She launched into a series of lectures about appropriate table manners and the importance of adhering to traditional social norms. Benedict, however, met her onslaught with a quiet resilience. He listened patiently, nodding occasionally, and even complimented her rather elaborate hat. He then subtly steered the conversation toward her extensive collection of vintage stamps, a topic that proved far more engaging than the proper way to hold a teacup.

The key to our success, I realized, wasn't about changing either of our worlds. It was about finding a way to bridge the chasm, to create a space where both could coexist, to celebrate the uniqueness of each while acknowledging their mutual connection. It was about embracing the messiness, the inevitable conflicts, the surprising moments of harmony.

The 'taming' project, initially conceived as a playful exploration of power dynamics, had evolved into something far deeper – a journey of understanding, mutual respect, and shared laughter. We had learned to appreciate the contrasts, to celebrate the idiosyncrasies, to find strength in our differences. It wasn't about conforming; it was about connection. It wasn't about control; it was about collaboration. It wasn't about taming; it was about understanding, embracing, and celebrating the wonderfully chaotic tapestry of life.

Our journey was a testament to the resilience of relationships, a
demonstration of the enduring power of

human connection. It was a testament to the fact that love isn't about changing the other person; it's about accepting them, flaws and all, and building a life together, amidst the inevitable chaos and the delightful surprises. It was, quite simply, a beautiful, messy, and utterly unforgettable adventure. And, of course, there was the ethicallysourced coffee. It played a surprisingly significant role.

We even started a small tradition: Friday night coffee tastings. This gave us a regular opportunity to debrief the week's social escapades, sharing anecdotes, laughing at our misadventures, and appreciating the simple pleasure of a perfectly brewed cup of coffee. It was a small ritual, a quiet testament to our journey, a reminder of how far we'd come, how much we'd learned, and how much more there was to discover together. The "taming" experiment, it seemed, had not only failed but spectacularly succeeded in ways neither of us could have ever predicted. The future, it seemed, held not the promise of a tamed individual, but a wonderfully unpredictable, vibrantly chaotic, and profoundly rewarding partnership. One that, I suspected, would involve a great deal more ethically-sourced coffee. And maybe a few more questionable sculptures made from garden gnomes.

ACCEPTANCE AND INCLUSION

The Friday night coffee tastings became a ritual, a sacred space where the battlefield of social integration morphed into a comfortable haven. Benedict, ever the pragmatist, meticulously documented the flavour profiles of each bean, charting their origins, roasting methods, and even the atmospheric pressure during brewing. My friends, meanwhile, used the opportunity to brainstorm their next collaborative art project – currently involving recycled plastic and a surprisingly large quantity of glitter. My family, surprisingly, had found a common ground in discussing the subtle nuances of different cream types. Who knew the intricacies of dairy farming could be so engaging?

Even Aunt Mildred, after a hesitant initial approach, found herself drawn into the weekly ritual. Initially, she'd appeared like a Victorian ghost, radiating disapproval from a plush armchair, her disapproval as stiff as her posture. But slowly, almost imperceptibly, she started to thaw. Benedict's quiet charm, his genuine interest in her opinions (even her less-than-progressive views on the role of women in modern society), chipped away at her formidable defenses. The shared enjoyment of a perfectly brewed cup of coffee, the comfortable camaraderie of the group, proved more powerful than any ingrained social prejudice.

One particularly memorable evening, Aunt Mildred surprised everyone by sharing a family anecdote about her own rebellious youth, a time when she'd secretly dyed her hair blue and attempted to learn the saxophone. The story was both endearing and surprisingly scandalous, revealing a side of her that had been hidden beneath layers of societal expectations and self-imposed constraints. It was a turning

point, a moment of genuine connection that transcended the superficial barriers of generation and ideology.

Penelope, ever the observer, noted that Aunt Mildred had actually smiled. A genuine, unforced smile, something rarely witnessed before. The smile, Penelope declared, was a clear indication that the integration process was finally complete. The battle, it seemed, had been won not through force, but through acceptance, understanding, and a shared appreciation for ethically sourced coffee.

This shared acceptance extended beyond

the weekly tastings. Benedict's spreadsheet obsession, initially a source of amusement and mild horror, had become a vital tool in navigating the complex social dynamics of our extended family and friends. It helped him predict potential flashpoints, suggesting appropriate conversational strategies, and even optimizing seating arrangements at larger gatherings. It was, in a strange way, a testament to the power of data-driven diplomacy.

My father, his initial apprehension about modern art now replaced with a curious fascination, had started attending Esme's art installations. He even admitted to appreciating the 'thought-provoking' nature of her work, a sentiment he delivered with a slightly bewildered expression but with genuine warmth. He had started attending Esme's art installations, even participating in a collaborative project involving found objects and repurposed garden tools. He declared this project to be a significant improvement on his garden gnome sculptures.

The inclusion extended to Barnaby's questionable fashion choices. Initially a source of constant amusement and occasional cringing from most of the group, Barnaby's outfits had become a source of friendly banter, each

ensemble sparking a spirited discussion about the intricacies of avantgarde style. It had turned into a running joke amongst the family, and surprisingly, Barnaby seemed to thrive in the acceptance. It didn't change his fashion sense, of course, but it certainly did alleviate his prior social anxiety.

Leo, always eager to engage in intellectual sparring, found himself surprisingly charmed by my mother's traditional values. Their discussions about organic versus hydroponic vegetables had evolved into thoughtful exchanges about sustainable living and environmental responsibility. They discovered a shared passion for preserving old family recipes, exchanging tips and techniques in a spirit of mutual respect and collaboration. My mother even started incorporating some of Leo's suggestions into her traditional family meals.

The most significant shift, however, occurred in my own perspective. My initial desire to "tame" Benedict had been born from a place of insecurity, a fear of vulnerability. But the process of blending our families and friends had forced me to confront my own preconceptions, to appreciate the rich tapestry of personalities and viewpoints within our group. I realized that "taming" wasn't about controlling or changing another person; it was about embracing the diversity of human experience, the beautiful chaos of life, and the power of connection.

The "taming" experiment, therefore, became

a testament to the beauty of imperfection. It wasn't about achieving a perfect, homogenous blend; it was about accepting and celebrating the unique qualities of each individual, building a strong foundation of mutual respect and understanding. We learned to navigate conflict with grace, to find common ground in seemingly irreconcilable differences, and to discover joy in the unpredictability of life.

The journey wasn't always easy. There were still occasional flare-ups, unexpected disagreements, and moments of utter social chaos. But these moments became less significant, less defining, dwarfed by the growing sense of belonging, the shared laughter, the deep-seated connections forged through shared experiences and a mutual appreciation for ethically-sourced coffee.

The final ingredient in this delightful concoction was the unshakeable support we all gave each other. It wasn't just about accepting the differences; it was about actively supporting each other in navigating them. It was about creating a space where everyone felt safe, respected, and valued, regardless of their background, their beliefs, or their eccentric hobbies.

The support manifested in many ways – a comforting word during a difficult moment, a helping hand during a stressful event, a shared laugh during a challenging interaction.

It was a silent promise to be present, to be supportive, to be a constant source of strength. It was the invisible glue that held our unconventional family and friends together, forging a bond that was stronger than any individual personality or belief system.

The "taming" experiment, therefore, was far from a failure. It was a spectacular success, proving that love wasn't about control, but about acceptance, understanding, and the unwavering support of a beautifully diverse and deeply connected group of individuals. And yes, ethically sourced coffee did play a rather significant role. It was, after all, the catalyst that brought us all together, the shared pleasure that solidified our unlikely alliance and served as a constant reminder of the journey we'd shared, the bonds we'd forged,

and the beautiful mess we'd created together. A mess, I might add, that was utterly and completely perfect.

HONEST CONVERSATIONS

The initial awkward silences, punctuated by the clinking of wine glasses and the nervous rustling of napkins, gradually dissolved into a comfortable rhythm of shared laughter and candid confessions. Benedict, surprisingly adept at navigating these uncharted waters of emotional intimacy, started by admitting his initial reservations about my family. He confessed that he'd envisioned a weekend of passive- aggressive glares, strained conversations, and the looming threat of a family feud worthy of a Shakespearean tragedy.

Instead, he'd found himself unexpectedly charmed by their eccentricities, their unyielding passion for their respective interests, and their surprising willingness to engage in his data-driven attempts at social harmony.

"I underestimated them," he conceded, a wry smile playing on his lips. "I thought I'd be deploying crisis management strategies all weekend. Instead, I found myself documenting the subtleties of family dynamics with the same meticulous attention I usually reserve for coffee bean roasting."

My own confession came next. I admitted to having initially viewed Benedict's spreadsheet-driven approach to family integration as a form of control, a subtle attempt to categorize and quantify the unpredictable nature of human relationships. It felt, to put it bluntly, deeply unromantic. The notion of a spreadsheet mediating our family gatherings seemed absurd. But I had been wrong.

"I apologize for being such a Luddite," I said, a touch of self- deprecating humor lacing my voice. "The truth is, your spreadsheets actually helped prevent several potential family

disasters. They're surprisingly effective at predicting flashpoints and suggesting tactful conversation starters."

Our conversation shifted towards the more challenging aspects of our newly blended lives. I acknowledged my own initial tendency to micromanage, a lingering echo of my attempts to 'tame' Benedict. He, in turn, confessed to having secretly enjoyed the initial challenge, finding my attempts at subtle manipulation both amusing and endearing. We both laughingly agreed that the "taming" process had been a two- way street, a mutual exploration of each other's strengths and weaknesses. It had been a game of mutual refinement, a fascinating, often comical, dance of personalities.

The conversation deepened, moving beyond the surface pleasantries to grapple with deeper issues. I confessed my initial anxieties about merging our vastly different worlds – his meticulously organized life versus my chaotic creativity. He acknowledged his own insecurities about navigating the complexities of my fiercely independent family and friends, their eclectic passions, and their unconventional approaches to social interaction. These candid exchanges, devoid of pretense or defensiveness, formed the bedrock of a new, deeper understanding.

We discussed my Aunt Mildred's remarkable transformation, her unexpected revelation of her rebellious youth acting as a symbol of the changing dynamics within our extended social circle. We talked about my father's surprising appreciation for Esme's avant-garde art and my mother's unexpected collaboration with Leo on the preservation of old family recipes.

"I never imagined my mother discussing hydroponics with Leo," I said, still amazed at the unexpected bonds that had

formed. "It's like witnessing a cultural exchange program in slow motion."

Benedict chuckled. "And to think it all started with a shared appreciation for ethically sourced coffee."

The honesty extended to our friends. Penelope, ever the insightful observer, offered her own assessment of the situation, her commentary laced with her trademark wit and sharp observations. Barnaby's acceptance into the fold, initially a cause of mild concern, had blossomed into a source of amusement and unexpected inspiration. His avant- garde fashion choices, once a source of apprehension, became a topic of playful banter, fostering a unique bond within the group. Esme, ever the catalyst for social change, contributed with her unique perspective, weaving her artistic insight into our ongoing conversations.

Leo, the perpetually engaged intellectual, provided a fresh lens through which we examined our evolving relationships, his insights both insightful and occasionally frustrating. His debates, while often intense, added a dimension of intellectual stimulation to our discussions, challenging our perspectives and prompting us to think more critically about our evolving relationships. His questions were insightful and probing, always challenging assumptions.

These conversations weren't always easy. There were moments of disagreement, occasional flare-ups of frustration, and instances where we stumbled over unspoken expectations. But the willingness to engage in open and honest dialogue, to address conflicts directly without resorting to passive-aggressiveness or evasion, transformed these moments of friction into opportunities for growth.

One particularly poignant conversation revolved around our differing approaches to conflict resolution. Benedict, ever the strategist, preferred a methodical, data-driven approach, outlining potential solutions and weighing the pros and cons of each option. I, on the other hand, tended towards a more emotional, intuitive approach, prioritizing empathy and understanding over logical analysis. Initially, these differences led to friction, but through honest conversation, we learned to appreciate the value of each approach. We learned to navigate the nuances of human relationships by combining our opposing strategies.

"I used to think that your data-driven approach was cold and impersonal," I admitted. "But I've come to appreciate its effectiveness in preventing unnecessary conflicts. It's like having a built-in conflict resolution algorithm."

Benedict smiled. "And I've learned that sometimes, the most effective solutions come not from spreadsheets and algorithms, but from empathy and understanding. Your emotional intelligence is my antidote to spreadsheet overload."

We had created a space where vulnerability was embraced rather than avoided, where imperfections were celebrated rather than condemned. We had learned the art of listening, the importance of empathy, and the unexpected beauty of constructive disagreement. The process of "taming," initially conceived as a playful challenge, had evolved into a profound journey of self-discovery and mutual growth. It wasn't about control; it was about understanding, acceptance, and a shared commitment to building a life together, flaws and all. We discovered that a beautifully imperfect blend of two distinct worlds didn't diminish either, but rather enhanced the beauty of each.

The honest conversations became our foundation, a continuous process of revealing, understanding, and building trust. These conversations were far from scripted, but far more valuable than any pre-determined narrative. They were the raw, unscripted moments of true intimacy, the moments where we truly saw and understood each other. They were, in their own unique way, a testament to the enduring power of honest communication, a power that transcended differences and forged a bond that felt stronger than ever before. The ability to communicate honestly, openly, and vulnerably - that was the true magic, far more potent than any attempt to 'tame' someone else. And in this mutual exploration of each other's hearts and minds, we discovered a love far more profound and fulfilling than we had ever imagined.

ACTIVE LISTENING

Our next significant step in this unconventional "taming" process involved a conscious effort to hone our active listening skills. It wasn't a sudden epiphany, but rather a gradual realization that true understanding wasn't about merely hearing words, but about truly *hearing* the person behind them. Benedict, with his characteristic methodical approach, suggested we start with a simple exercise: we would each take turns recounting a significant event from our past, focusing on the emotions involved rather than just the facts. My initial reaction was a mixture of amusement and skepticism. An exercise in emotional excavation? It sounded suspiciously like therapy.

"Don't worry," Benedict reassured me, sensing my apprehension. "It's not about dredging up old traumas. It's about understanding each other's emotional landscapes."

He started first, recounting a childhood memory of a disastrous science fair project involving a malfunctioning volcano and a

THE TAMING OF THE MAN

catastrophic eruption of baking soda and vinegar. He spoke not just of the technical failure, but of the crushing disappointment he felt, the sting of public humiliation, and the unexpected comfort he found in his grandfather's quiet support. I listened intently, not just to the narrative but to the subtle shifts in his tone, the fleeting expressions that crossed his face, the unspoken emotions that lingered beneath the surface. I found myself surprised by the vulnerability he displayed, a vulnerability that contrasted sharply with his usually composed demeanor.

My turn was more challenging. I chose to recount a particularly intense argument with my mother, a clash of

wills that had left me feeling both frustrated and heartbroken. I spoke of the simmering resentment, the feeling of being misunderstood, the desperate need for validation. As I spoke, I became acutely aware of Benedict's undivided attention. He didn't interrupt, didn't offer unsolicited advice, simply listened, his gaze unwavering, his expression reflecting empathy and understanding. He wasn't just hearing my words; he was absorbing my emotions, experiencing them alongside me.

This exercise became a regular practice, a sacred ritual in our evolving relationship. We would share our triumphs and frustrations, our anxieties and aspirations, our hopes and fears, always striving for deeper levels of understanding. The focus was less on resolving conflicts and more on fostering a sense of emotional intimacy, a feeling of being truly seen and heard.

One evening, over a pot of strong Earl Grey tea, Benedict confessed to a surprising difficulty in actively listening to his own mother. She, a whirlwind of relentless energy and opinions, often overwhelmed him with her rapid-fire monologues. He struggled to disentangle the core message from the verbal torrent.

"It's not that I don't care," he explained, his voice tinged with frustration. "It's just... I get lost in the noise."

I understood completely. I've encountered similar challenges with my Aunt Mildred, whose pronouncements on the state of the nation often overshadowed the actual points she was trying to make. We brainstormed strategies for navigating these conversation maelstroms, focusing on techniques like summarizing key points, asking clarifying questions, and subtly guiding the conversation towards calmer waters.

Over time, our active listening skills improved dramatically. We learned to discern the unspoken messages behind words, the subtle cues in body language, the emotional undercurrents that often dictated the true meaning of a conversation. We learned to distinguish between factual statements and emotional expressions, to identify our own biases and preconceived notions, and to approach each conversation with a genuine desire to understand, rather than to be understood.

This wasn't always easy. There were times when our differences in communication styles created friction. Benedict, with his logical mind, sometimes struggled with my more emotional approach, while I occasionally found his systematic approach to conversations overly clinical. But the key was our willingness to engage in open dialogue about these challenges, to acknowledge our shortcomings, and to celebrate our individual strengths.

One memorable evening, a heated discussion about the merits of vintage versus modern furniture escalated into a full-blown argument. I, a passionate advocate for the charm of antique pieces, found myself emotionally overwhelmed by Benedict's pragmatic arguments about durability and practicality. The conversation teetered on the brink of a full- blown disagreement, punctuated by sharp retorts and exasperated sighs.

But then, something shifted. Benedict paused, took a deep breath, and said, "I think I'm missing something here. Tell me again why these old chairs are so important to you."

He didn't dismiss my feelings; he simply expressed a desire to understand them. And in that moment, I realized that his request was more than just a question. It was an act of deep listening.

I explained my emotional connection to the chairs, the memories they held, the sense of history they evoked, the way they reflected my own appreciation for the past. As I spoke, Benedict listened attentively, his eyes conveying a genuine desire to understand. When I finished, he apologized for his initial dismissal of my feelings, acknowledging that he'd focused too much on the logical arguments and not enough on the emotional significance of the objects.

This incident became a turning point in our journey towards effective communication. We realized that the ability to listen actively wasn't simply about hearing the words, but about embracing the emotional context, acknowledging the underlying emotions, and understanding the perspective of the other person. It wasn't about winning arguments or proving points; it was about fostering a deeper connection.

Active listening became more than just a communication skill; it became a symbol of our evolving relationship, a testament to our willingness to engage with each other on a deeper, more emotional level. It was about cultivating a space where vulnerability was celebrated, imperfections were embraced, and honest communication was valued above all else.

This journey of active listening extended beyond our immediate relationship, influencing the way we interacted with our friends and families. We encouraged others to adopt similar practices, sharing insights and techniques gleaned from our own experiences. We observed how this shift in communication style impacted interactions within our broader social circle, leading to clearer understanding, reduced conflict, and stronger bonds.

Our friends, initially skeptical, were eventually won over. Penelope, a master of witty repartee, found that active listening actually enhanced her ability to deliver her perfectly crafted barbs, ensuring they landed with the intended impact and not as unintentional insults. Barnaby, always eager to express his unique style, learned to present his often unconventional ideas in a more accessible way.

Even Leo, the intellectually restless debater, realized that active listening improved his ability to engage in meaningful dialogue, fostering more enriching discussions.

As our practice of active listening matured, we realized it was more than a mere technique. It was a philosophy, a way of being. It wasn't just about hearing words; it was about embracing the entire human experience, with all its complexities, contradictions, and emotional nuances. It taught us patience, empathy, and the profound importance of genuine connection. The process of "taming," once a playful challenge, had transformed into a beautiful journey of mutual growth, grounded in the enduring power of communication. And in this, we found not just a stronger relationship, but a deeper understanding of ourselves and each other. The art of truly listening – this, we discovered, was the key to unlocking the heart's truest language.

RESOLVING CONFLICTS

Our journey towards mastering communication wasn't solely about the quiet art of listening; it was about proactively navigating the inevitable storms of disagreement. We discovered that conflict, far from being an enemy, could actually be a fertile ground for growth, a catalyst for deeper understanding if approached with the right tools. Our initial attempts were, to put it mildly, clumsy. Remember the incident with the antique chairs? That was a fairly gentle skirmish compared to the battles that followed.

One particularly memorable conflict erupted during a weekend trip to a quaint, yet decidedly overpriced, seaside village. The argument, seemingly innocuous at first, began with a debate over the merits of various seafood restaurants. Benedict, ever the pragmatist, favoured a highly-rated establishment boasting five-star reviews and an extensive wine list. I, captivated by the charm of a tiny, family-run trattoria with peeling paint and questionable hygiene standards, countered with an impassioned plea for authentic, albeit potentially questionable, culinary adventure.

The initial disagreement quickly escalated. Benedict's methodical approach to decision-making, his insistence on quantifiable data and objective assessments clashed head-on with my more intuitive, emotionally driven preferences. He presented graphs and charts comparing customer ratings and prices. I responded with evocative descriptions of the seaside charm, the potential for serendipitous encounters, and the undeniable allure of culinary risk. The air crackled with tension, punctuated by pointed remarks and increasingly sarcastic retorts.

This, however, was where our training in active listening truly began to bear fruit. We paused. We didn't shout over each other, didn't storm off in a huff. Instead, we employed the strategies we'd developed: summarizing each other's perspectives, identifying the underlying needs and desires beneath the surface arguments, and focusing on the emotional core of the disagreement.

Benedict, after a moment of thoughtful silence, admitted that his desire for a flawless dining experience stemmed from a need for predictability and control. He craved the assurance of a safe, reliable option, a sanctuary from the unexpected chaos that often punctuated his life. I, in turn, confessed that my attraction to the trattoria wasn't just about the food; it was about embracing the element of surprise, the possibility of discovering something unique and unexpected, a reflection of my own adventurous spirit.

Once we understood the underlying emotions, the conflict deflated. It wasn't about choosing between one restaurant or the other; it was about acknowledging and respecting each other's differing needs and preferences. We compromised, opting for a slightly less high-brow establishment that offered a blend of reliability and a touch of adventure. The meal, it turned out, was quite delightful.

This experience taught us a crucial lesson: effective conflict resolution wasn't about winning or losing, but about finding common ground, understanding the emotional landscape, and meeting each other halfway. We developed a series of strategies to prevent misunderstandings from escalating into full-blown arguments. We learned to identify triggers, to recognise subtle signs of rising tension, and to pre-empt arguments before they could fully ignite.

One particularly effective technique involved what we termed "emotional pre-emptive strikes." If either of us sensed a disagreement brewing, we'd proactively address the issue before it could fester. This involved a clear and concise statement of our feelings, articulated without blame or accusation. For example, instead of launching into a tirade about Benedict's habitual lateness, I might say something like, "I've noticed you've been running late recently, and it makes me feel a little anxious and undervalued." This direct, yet non-accusatory approach allowed for open communication without triggering a defensive reaction.

Another crucial aspect involved establishing clear boundaries. We learned to articulate our individual needs and preferences without judgment or criticism. This involved understanding our own emotional limits and setting healthy boundaries to protect our emotional wellbeing. For instance, I established a boundary around unnecessary criticism of my work, explaining to Benedict that while his feedback was valued, constant negative critique undermined my confidence and

creativity. Similarly, Benedict established a boundary around interruptions during his focused work periods.

Our conflict resolution methods weren't perfect; there were still occasions when tensions flared and tempers frayed. But the key difference was our ability to recover gracefully, to acknowledge our mistakes, to apologize sincerely, and to recommit to our shared goals of mutual respect and understanding. We learned to use disagreements as opportunities for learning, growth, and strengthening our bond.

Moreover, our approach to conflict resolution extended beyond our personal relationship. We found ourselves applying similar principles in our interactions with friends,

family, and colleagues. The ability to listen actively, to identify underlying emotions, and to approach disagreements with empathy transformed our communication style in all aspects of our lives.

Penelope, for instance, who had once prided herself on her ability to deliver cutting remarks with laser-like precision, discovered that active listening allowed her to deploy her wit with more intention and less sting. By understanding the emotional context of her interactions, she could tailor her responses to achieve a desired effect without causing unnecessary hurt.

Barnaby, a whirlwind of ideas and often impulsive pronouncements, learned to articulate his thoughts with greater clarity and sensitivity. He discovered that by actively listening to the responses of others, he could refine his arguments and avoid unnecessary misunderstandings. Even Leo, the intellectual sparring partner, acknowledged that active listening enhanced his ability to engage in stimulating debate without descending into unproductive conflict.

Our journey of "taming" – a playful yet

profound endeavor – had fundamentally transformed our understanding of communication. It was no longer about control or domination, but about partnership, mutual growth, and the delicate art of navigating the complexities of human interaction. We realized that true intimacy wasn't about the absence of conflict, but about the ability to resolve conflict effectively and emerge stronger and more connected than before. The power of communication, we discovered, wasn't just about expressing ourselves; it was about truly understanding each other. And that, we realised, was the most potent form of connection. The seemingly simple act of truly listening transformed not just our relationship, but our lives.

EXPRESSING EMOTIONS

The ability to articulate our emotions, to lay bare our vulnerabilities without fear of judgment, proved to be the cornerstone of our evolving relationship. It wasn't a sudden epiphany, but a gradual process of unlearning ingrained societal expectations and embracing a new paradigm of emotional honesty. For me, this involved dismantling years of conditioning that had taught me to suppress my feelings, to present a façade of stoic independence, a carefully constructed persona that hid the tempestuous sea of emotions churning beneath the surface. Benedict, on the other hand, wrestled with a different set of challenges – a tendency to intellectualize his feelings, to bury his emotions under a layer of logic and reason, often avoiding direct emotional expression.

Our initial attempts at emotional vulnerability were tentative, almost clumsy. We started small, sharing seemingly insignificant details about our day – a minor frustration at work, a fleeting moment of joy, a surprising encounter with a particularly grumpy squirrel. These seemingly inconsequential moments provided a safe space to explore the landscape of our emotions, to experiment with expressing feelings without the pressure of grand pronouncements or dramatic confessions.

One evening, while curled up on the sofa with a mug of chamomile tea (a ritual we'd adopted during our quieter moments), I confessed my anxieties about my upcoming book deadline. The weight of expectation, the fear of failure, the self-doubt that gnawed at my confidence – I laid it all bare, the words tumbling out in a torrent of confession. Benedict listened, not with the detached politeness of a

bystander, but with the genuine concern of a partner. He didn't offer solutions or platitudes; he simply validated my feelings, acknowledging the legitimacy of my anxieties and offering quiet support. It was in that moment, amidst the shared silence and the comforting warmth of the tea, that I understood the transformative power of emotional vulnerability.

His own journey toward emotional openness was more gradual.

Benedict, a creature of logic and order, initially struggled to articulate his feelings, preferring the language of data and analysis to the messy complexities of emotion.

However, as he witnessed my willingness to

share my vulnerabilities, he gradually began to emulate my behaviour. He started sharing his frustrations with work projects, his anxieties about the future, his moments of self-doubt. It wasn't always easy; he often stumbled over his words, his sentences laced with hesitant qualifiers and apologetic disclaimers. But the effort itself, the willingness to break down the emotional barriers he'd erected around himself, was a testament to the growth we were experiencing together.

We discovered that expressing emotions wasn't always a comfortable process. There were tears, both of sadness and joy, moments of anger and frustration, occasions when the raw emotion threatened to overwhelm us. But amidst the vulnerability, we found a deeper level of intimacy, a connection that transcended the superficial niceties of polite conversation. We learned to navigate the complexities of emotional expression with grace and empathy, acknowledging that it was okay to feel a range of emotions, even the ones that were less socially acceptable. We learned to embrace the messy reality of human emotions, to view them not as weaknesses to be overcome, but as integral parts of our shared human experience.

One particularly poignant moment occurred during a visit to my family. A long-standing tension between my mother and me unexpectedly resurfaced, triggering a wave of intense emotion. Instead of retreating into silence or engaging in a combative exchange,

I allowed myself to express my hurt and frustration openly, sharing my feelings with Benedict.

He listened, offering words of support and validation, and helped me process the complex emotions swirling within me. It was a powerful moment, one that underscored the importance of emotional expression not just within our relationship, but also as a tool for navigating the complexities of our family dynamics.

This newfound emotional openness wasn't limited to our personal relationship. It seeped into every facet of our lives, affecting our interactions with friends, family, and colleagues. We were more empathetic, more understanding, more tolerant of others' vulnerabilities. We learned to approach disagreements with greater compassion, understanding that often, behind sharp words and defensive posturing lay a wellspring of hurt or fear. We found ourselves offering more support, more encouragement, more genuine understanding. The transformation wasn't sudden or dramatic, but a slow, gradual shift in perspective, a quiet revolution in how we interacted with the world and with each other.

The ability to express emotions, to share our vulnerabilities, proved to be the most potent form of communication, the glue that bound our relationship together. It wasn't a matter of avoiding conflict but of navigating it with emotional intelligence and grace. We realized that true connection wasn't about achieving perfect emotional harmony but about creating a safe space where we could express ourselves authentically, where our vulnerabilities were embraced, and

where our emotions, however tumultuous, were met with understanding and compassion. This mutual vulnerability became the bedrock of our relationship, a testament to the transformative power of honest communication and emotional openness. It was in this shared vulnerability, in the quiet acknowledgment of our imperfections, that we found a deeper, more profound connection than we could ever have imagined. We had found a way, amidst the chaos of modern life, to create a haven of understanding, a testament to the enduring power of human connection. And that, perhaps, was the greatest triumph of all. The "taming," if one could even call it that, wasn't about control or conformity; it was about a shared journey of emotional discovery, a mutual embrace of vulnerability, and the cultivation of a love built on the foundation of true, unfiltered communication. It was a love story, not of subjugation, but of shared growth, a testament to the power of open hearts and honest words. The journey, far from being over, had only just begun.

STRENGTHENING
THE BOND

The quiet hum of domesticity had settled over our lives, a comforting counterpoint to the previously chaotic symphony of misunderstandings. The ability to communicate, to truly *see* each other, wasn't just about exchanging words; it was about deciphering the unspoken language of gestures, silences, and the subtle shifts in expression. We'd moved beyond the superficial pleasantries, the carefully constructed narratives designed to avoid conflict. Now, our conversations were richer, more nuanced, peppered with both laughter and the occasional, healthy dose of bickering. But even the arguments felt different, infused with a newfound understanding that underpinned even our disagreements.

Remember those early days, when a simple request for a cup of tea could escalate into a full-blown philosophical debate on the merits of Earl Grey versus Darjeeling? Those days felt like a distant memory, replaced by a more fluid, intuitive understanding of each other's needs. Now, a simple glance across the kitchen could convey the same message, a shared understanding that transcended the need for explicit articulation. It wasn't that we had eliminated conflict; life, after all, is far too messy for that utopian ideal. Instead, we'd learned to navigate those inevitable clashes with a grace and maturity that surprised even ourselves.

One evening, as we were preparing dinner (Benedict, surprisingly, had embraced his inner domestic god, mastering the art of risotto with admirable dexterity), a minor disagreement erupted. It started with a seemingly innocuous comment about the placement of the spice rack – a detail of such microscopic insignificance that it would have previously
sparked a full-scale battle of wills. But this time,

the conversation unfolded differently. Instead of launching into accusatory rhetoric, we paused, took a breath, and attempted to articulate our underlying concerns. For Benedict, it was about order and efficiency – the spice rack, in his view, needed to be strategically placed for optimal culinary flow. For me, it was about the aesthetics, the visual harmony of the kitchen. It wasn't about the spice rack at all, but about our differing approaches to organization and aesthetics. Once we'd acknowledged the root of our disagreement, the absurdity of the argument melted away, replaced by laughter and a shared understanding. We compromised, of course, finding a solution that satisfied both our aesthetic and logistical needs. The spice rack, ultimately, remained a testament to our newfound ability to negotiate and compromise.

This improved communication wasn't confined to domestic squabbles. It permeated every facet of our lives, shaping our interactions with friends, family, and even our respective work colleagues. I noticed a shift in how I dealt with the relentless pressure of deadlines and the constant demands of my writing career. Before, I would retreat into a silent fortress of solitude, nursing my anxieties in isolation. Now, I shared my struggles with Benedict, allowing him to offer support, not in the form of empty platitudes, but through practical actions: bringing me tea, offering to take care of household chores, simply listening without judgment. He, in turn, found a new level of openness in discussing his own professional challenges, sharing his frustrations and successes with a level of vulnerability I had not previously witnessed.

The difference was profound. Sharing my worries didn't weaken me; it strengthened me, forging a deeper connection with Benedict. His willingness to listen, to validate my feelings without attempting to "fix" them, was a revelation.

He discovered that his support was more

effective when it came in the form of empathy rather than solutions. The old adage, "A problem shared is a problem halved," held truer than ever. The burden of carrying my anxieties alone was lifted, replaced by the shared weight of our mutual support. The mutual sharing of anxieties and daily frustrations began to take on the air of a shared ritual, a comforting routine that strengthened the bond between us. It created a space for us to be vulnerable, imperfect, and wholly human.

This wasn't a sudden, magical transformation; it was a gradual evolution, a conscious choice to prioritize communication and understanding over avoidance and conflict. It required patience, empathy, and a willingness to continuously learn and grow together. We stumbled, of course, we fell, and there were moments when frustration threatened to overwhelm us. But through it all, we held onto the thread of communication, the shared belief that open dialogue was the key to navigating the complexities of our relationship.

We started incorporating regular "check-in" sessions, dedicated time for open communication, devoid of distractions. These weren't formal therapy sessions, but informal conversations where we discussed our feelings, our anxieties, our hopes, and our dreams. Sometimes, these conversations were infused with laughter; other times, they were emotionally charged, revealing unspoken vulnerabilities and long-held fears. But always, they were an affirmation of our commitment to mutual understanding, a celebration of our willingness to unravel the intricate tapestry of our shared lives. These quiet moments of introspection and vulnerability proved to be some of the most meaningful and intimate moments in our evolving relationship. They were the spaces in which we truly saw each other.

These honest conversations weren't always easy. There were moments of intense emotion, tears, and the raw exposure of our vulnerabilities. But in those moments of shared vulnerability, we discovered a deeper level of intimacy, a connection that transcended the superficial pleasantries and polite formalities that had once defined our interactions. It was in these emotionally charged moments that we revealed the true strength of our partnership, discovering that our love was not predicated on superficial compatibility or harmonious agreement but on our mutual willingness to navigate the complexities of our shared existence. We found strength and support in each other's vulnerabilities, and in the process, learned that true love resided in the capacity to understand and embrace each other's imperfections.

The impact of this deepened communication extended beyond our immediate relationship, subtly influencing our interactions with the world at large. We found ourselves more empathetic towards others, more understanding of their struggles, more tolerant of their imperfections. We became better communicators, not only with each other but also with friends, family, and colleagues. We learned to approach disagreements with a newfound sensitivity, recognizing the underlying emotions that frequently fuelled conflict and conflict avoidance. The ability to truly listen, to truly hear, transformed our relationships. We were no longer just reacting to events but actively participating in shaping them, crafting a narrative that celebrated our shared experiences and mutual growth.

This newfound strength, this deeper connection, wasn't a destination but a journey, an ongoing process of learning, growth, and mutual understanding. The "taming," if one could even call it that, was less about control and more about collaboration, a mutual evolution of two individuals

committed to building a life filled with honest communication, shared vulnerabilities, and a profound sense of mutual respect. The journey wasn't over; it was, in fact, just beginning, a testament to the enduring power of love, vulnerability, and the transformative power of open communication. It was a journey towards a more authentic, more fulfilling partnership, built on the solid foundations of trust, understanding, and a shared commitment to continuous growth. And that,

AUREALIA NELSON

perhaps, was the greatest love story of all.

PERSONAL GROWTH

The transformation wasn't solely confined to our relationship; it extended into our individual lives, a ripple effect emanating from the heart of our evolving partnership. For me, the change was palpable in my writing. Before, my work, while successful, often felt... hollow. A clever construct, meticulously crafted, but lacking a certain emotional depth, a genuine connection to the human experience. My characters, though witty and sharp-tongued, remained distant, unreachable, their motivations often dictated by plot rather than genuine emotional turmoil. I'd been so focused on the cleverness of the prose, the intricate plotting, that I'd neglected the heart of the story – the raw, messy, beautiful messiness of human emotion.

But something shifted. The newfound openness and vulnerability in my relationship with Benedict seeped into my creative process. I found myself writing with a newfound honesty, exploring themes of insecurity, fear, and vulnerability with a frankness I hadn't dared to embrace before. My characters became richer, more nuanced, their motivations driven by genuine human needs and desires, their struggles reflective of the complexities I was navigating in my own life.

I started to incorporate elements of my own experiences into my stories, not in a literal sense, but in the emotional core of the narrative. The anxieties I'd previously hidden away, the fears I'd carefully suppressed, found their way onto the page, transformed into the struggles of my fictional characters.

This wasn't about self-indulgent navel-gazing; it was about authenticity, about tapping into a wellspring of emotion that had previously remained untapped. The stories became more personal, more visceral, resonating with readers on a deeper level than ever before. My work, for the first time, felt truly *mine*, infused with the essence of my experiences and the lessons I was learning in love and life.

Reviews started reflecting this shift. Critics lauded the emotional depth of my work, praising the honesty and vulnerability that permeated my narratives. My readers responded with an outpouring of support, sharing their own stories, their own struggles, their own triumphs. The connection felt profound, a testament to the power of genuine storytelling. It wasn't just about the words on the page; it was about the shared human experience, the universal language of emotion that transcended the boundaries of fiction and reality. The success was gratifying, but more importantly, it was a validation of my personal growth, a reflection of the transformative power of self- discovery within the context of a loving, supportive relationship.

Benedict, too, underwent a significant personal transformation. He'd always been a capable man, successful in his career, yet he'd often suppressed his emotions, maintaining a façade of stoicism that masked a deep-seated insecurity. He confided in me about his anxieties regarding his career, his fears of failure, his anxieties about not meeting expectations – both his own and those of others. The initial reluctance to express these feelings was palpable, but the gradual erosion of his defensive mechanisms revealed a vulnerability that was both touching and surprisingly attractive.

His professional life underwent a significant shift as well. He'd been working tirelessly, driven by an almost obsessive need to prove himself, neglecting his personal well-being in the process. But with the newfound clarity and support that

came from our stronger communication, he began to re- evaluate his priorities. He realised the importance of balance, of setting boundaries, of cherishing his personal life alongside his career aspirations.

He started to say "no" more often, to prioritize his well-being over external pressures. He began to delegate tasks, to trust his team, to acknowledge his own limitations without fear of judgment. His work became more focused, more creative, less burdened by the weight of self-imposed pressure. His leadership style softened, becoming more collaborative and less autocratic. His success remained, but it was now grounded in a more balanced, sustainable approach to life, an approach informed by the lessons he'd learned through our shared journey of personal growth.

This wasn't about changing who he was, but about embracing a more authentic version of himself. The man he had been, whilst undeniably capable and successful, lacked the emotional depth, the nuanced selfawareness that emerged from this profound relationship. His personal growth was not a rejection of his previous self, but an expansion, a fuller blossoming of his potential. He found a quiet strength in vulnerability, a confidence born not from arrogance but from a deep understanding of his own strengths and weaknesses.

Our shared journey of personal growth had an undeniable impact on our relationship. We'd moved beyond the initial playful sparring, the attempts at "taming" each other. The "taming" had been nothing more than a clumsy metaphor, a playful exploration of power dynamics that ultimately led to a deeper understanding of our own needs and insecurities.

The laughter remained, the banter continued, but it was infused with a newfound depth, a shared understanding that

transcended the superficial. Our arguments, when they did occur, were less about control and more about communication, a willingness to hear each other's perspectives, to find common ground, to appreciate our differences. The spice rack, once a battleground, now stood as a quiet testament to our shared journey, a reminder of how easily trivial issues could be resolved when underpinned by a foundation of trust, mutual respect, and understanding.

We learned the art of compromise, not as a defeat but as a creative act, a testament to our ability to find solutions that honored our individual needs while strengthening our bond. We had learned the art of effective conflict resolution, understanding that even disagreements could serve as an opportunity to learn and grow together, moving beyond mere resolutions to forging deeper understandings of each other's motivations and needs. The process became not one of "winning" an argument, but of cultivating our partnership through mutual respect and collaboration.

Our journey wasn't without its challenges, its occasional stumbles. There were moments of doubt, of frustration, of the overwhelming urge to retreat into old patterns of avoidance. But through it all, we clung to the thread of communication, the commitment to honesty and vulnerability. We had learned to embrace the messiness of life, to find beauty in our imperfections, to celebrate the unique tapestry of our evolving partnership.

In the end, the "taming" had been a self-imposed myth, a narrative we had both consciously (and often unconsciously) constructed. What remained was a genuine connection, a deep and abiding love that flourished not through control but through growth, through understanding, through the transformative power of honest communication. And that, far from being a taming, was a liberation, for both of us. It

was the kind of love story that didn't need a happily ever after; it was a happily ever becoming, a testament to the enduring power of a love built on mutual respect, continuous growth, and a healthy dose of shared laughter.

SHARED ASPIRATIONS

The quiet hum of the evening settled around us, a comfortable blanket woven from the shared silence of contentment. We sat on the sofa, the remnants of a surprisingly amicable debate over the merits of artisanal cheese still lingering in the air. It wasn't the cheese itself, of course, that had sparked the discussion; it was the underlying principle – the meticulous planning, the dedication to craft, the willingness to invest time and effort into something beyond the mundane. This, we realized, was a metaphor for our lives together.

Benedict, surprisingly, was the one who articulated it first. He'd been unusually quiet after work, a stillness that had initially concerned me, but which now, in the soft glow of the lamplight, felt infused with a profound sense of contemplation. He spoke of his future, not in terms of career milestones or material possessions – things that had previously dominated his narrative – but in terms of experiences, of shared adventures, of creating a life rich in meaning and purpose.

"I've been thinking," he began, his voice low and thoughtful, "about what I truly want. Not just professionally, but... everything." He paused, fiddling with a loose thread on the sofa cushion, a nervous habit I'd come to associate with moments of profound reflection. "And I realize... it's not about climbing the corporate ladder anymore. It's about building something lasting, something... meaningful."

His words resonated deeply within me. For so long, his ambition had felt like a separate entity, a powerful force that often overshadowed our shared life. But now, his ambition

felt... integrated, interwoven with our shared aspirations. He wasn't talking about individual achievement; he was speaking of a *we*, a collaborative effort directed toward a common goal.

"Me too," I said, feeling a rush of warmth, a sense of profound connection. "I've been reevaluating things, too. Not just my writing, but... everything. The relentless pursuit of success... it feels hollow now, without a deeper meaning. It used to feel like a race, but now... it feels like a journey."

And that's how we began to define our shared aspirations. It wasn't a formal agreement, drawn up on legal paper, but a gentle unfolding of our desires, a mutual agreement reached through quiet contemplation and heartfelt conversations. We talked about travel – not luxurious vacations in exotic locales, but backpacking trips through remote landscapes, immersing ourselves in different cultures, experiencing the raw beauty of the world. We envisioned ourselves learning new languages, sharing the experience of mastering something together, the subtle satisfaction of growing in tandem.

We discussed writing projects, collaborative efforts where we could meld our individual talents to create something truly unique. I envisioned us co-writing a screenplay, combining his sharp, analytical mind with my imaginative storytelling. He suggested we collaborate on a historical fiction novel, blending his meticulous research skills with my flair for descriptive language. The possibilities felt endless, a boundless canvas upon which we could paint the masterpiece of our shared creative vision.

We also talked about our desire for a family, a topic I had previously approached with hesitancy, fearing it would disrupt the delicate balance we'd carefully cultivated. But

this time, it felt different. The fear had dissipated, replaced by a sense of excitement, a shared longing for the joy and challenges of parenthood. We weren't discussing babies as a means of fulfilling societal expectations; we were envisioning the creation of a family unit, a loving environment where we could nurture a child's growth and development, sharing the experiences that would shape their life.

Our conversations extended beyond the grand aspirations, delving into the mundane details of daily life. We talked about buying a small cottage in the countryside, a place where we could escape the relentless pace of city life, and where we could cultivate a garden – a tangible representation of our shared growth and nurturing tendencies. We imagined lazy Sundays spent tending to our plants, the quiet satisfaction of watching seeds sprout and bloom.

We even discussed the seemingly trivial aspects of our life. The routine of preparing dinner together, the shared responsibility of household chores, the simple pleasure of watching a movie snuggled on the sofa – all these moments, once overlooked, were now viewed as integral parts of our shared tapestry, the threads that weaved together the rich texture of our lives. The spice rack, once a symbol of our initial conflict, now symbolized the collaborative effort to create a harmonious home.

These weren't just aspirations; they were commitments, a quiet affirmation of our willingness to work together, to support each other's dreams, to navigate life's challenges hand-in-hand. It wasn't about achieving individual goals; it was about sharing the journey, the triumphs, and even the occasional stumbles, along the way.

It wasn't a perfect picture, of course. There were still moments of disagreement, of friction, of the inevitable clash of personalities. But the difference was profound. These moments no longer felt like battles to be won or lost; they were opportunities for growth, for deeper understanding, for strengthening the foundation of our partnership.

We learned to communicate more effectively, to listen without interrupting, to express our needs without resorting to blame or resentment. We discovered the art of compromise, a skill that required us to step outside of our individual comfort zones, to relinquish the need to always be right, to prioritize the well-being of our relationship over the satisfaction of winning an argument.

We both realised that "taming" had never been about control; it had been about learning to communicate, to understand, to build a life together that honored both our individual strengths and aspirations. The process had transformed us, shaping us into better versions of ourselves, individuals capable of navigating the complexities of a modern relationship with grace, humor, and a profound sense of love and mutual respect.

Our shared aspirations extended beyond the personal sphere. We discussed our desire to make a positive impact on the world, to contribute something meaningful to society. We considered volunteering our time to a local charity, or using our skills and talents to support causes we were passionate about. The idea of philanthropy wasn't simply a charitable act; it was a reflection of our shared values, a commitment to use our success to help others. We talked about the importance of environmental consciousness, about living a sustainable life, about leaving a positive legacy for future generations. These weren't simply grand pronouncements;

they were the building blocks of a life lived with intention, purpose, and a profound sense of shared responsibility.

This commitment to shared aspirations, this shared journey toward a meaningful future, transformed our relationship. It wasn't just about love; it was about partnership, collaboration, and mutual respect. The laughter, the banter, the occasional disagreements – all of it was infused with a deeper meaning, a shared understanding that transcended the superficial, reaching into the very heart of our shared purpose.

Our journey wasn't complete, of course. Life, as we both knew, is a continuous process of growth and change. But we had found something extraordinary – a foundation built on mutual respect, shared values, and a commitment to build a life together, one filled with love, laughter, and the endless possibilities of a future we would create, side by side. And that, we both realized, was far more fulfilling than any fairy tale ending. It was a story of becoming, of constant evolution, of a love that grew stronger with every shared experience, every challenge overcome, every shared aspiration realized. It was, in its own unique way, the perfect happily ever after.

OVERCOMING CHALLENGES

The following months weren't a seamless progression of idyllic domesticity, of course. Life, even with its carefully constructed shared aspirations, had a habit of throwing curveballs. One such curveball arrived in the form of Benedict's unexpected redundancy. The news hit him like a ton of bricks, leaving him reeling, his carefully constructed sense of self momentarily shattered. He'd spent years climbing the corporate ladder, identifying himself so completely with his professional achievements that his sense of worth felt inextricably linked to his position. The loss of his job, therefore, felt like a profound personal failure.

Initially, his reaction was a retreat into silence, a sullen withdrawal from our carefully constructed bubble of shared happiness. He wandered through the house like a ghost, his usual vibrant energy replaced by a listless apathy. He avoided conversations, his eyes fixed on some distant, internal landscape of despair. I watched him, my heart aching with a mixture of empathy and frustration. This was the man I had patiently, albeit playfully, attempted to "tame," the man who had finally begun to understand the nuances of a shared life, a life where individual aspirations were woven into a larger tapestry of shared purpose. And yet, here he was, unravelling at the seams.

My initial impulse was to fix it, to wave my magic wand of emotional support and somehow magically erase his despair. But I knew that wouldn't work. This wasn't a problem to be solved; it was a process to be navigated, a journey of self- discovery that he had to undertake on his own. So, I adjusted my approach. I stopped trying to fix him, and instead, I focused on supporting him.

I listened patiently to his anxieties, validating his feelings without minimizing his pain. I didn't offer platitudes or simplistic solutions; instead, I offered unwavering empathy, a silent presence that allowed him to process his emotions without judgment. I reminded him of his strengths, of the myriad talents and skills that extended far beyond his corporate role. I reminded him of his values, his commitment to meaningful purpose, a purpose that extended far beyond the confines of a single job.

And then, I waited. I waited for him to emerge from his self- imposed exile, to rediscover his own resilience, to reclaim his sense of self. It wasn't easy. There were moments of intense frustration, of wanting to shake him out of his despair, to force him to see the light at the end of the tunnel. But I held back, remembering that true support wasn't about rescuing someone from their struggles; it was about empowering them to navigate those struggles themselves.

Slowly, almost imperceptibly, a shift began to occur. He started to emerge from his shell, his conversations becoming less hesitant, his laughter returning, albeit in muted tones. He began to explore new avenues, to reconnect with old passions he'd neglected in the relentless pursuit of corporate success. He rediscovered his love of photography, his talent for creative writing, his passion for historical research. He started volunteering at a local museum, immersing himself in the world of history, connecting with others who shared his passion.

His redundancy, initially perceived as a devastating blow, became a catalyst for growth, a pivotal moment that forced him to re-evaluate his priorities, his values, his sense of self. He realized that his worth wasn't defined by his job title or his salary; it was defined by his character, his talents, his

contributions to the world. He discovered a hidden resilience, a strength he hadn't known he possessed. He emerged from the experience not just stronger, but transformed, his perspective broadened, his sense of purpose deepened.

Our shared aspirations, previously a distant dream, became more tangible, more achievable. His newfound freedom from the constraints of corporate life allowed him to dedicate more time to our shared creative projects. We began working on a screenplay together, his analytical mind complementing my imaginative storytelling. The process wasn't always harmonious – creative differences inevitably arose, sparking lively debates and the occasional playful argument. But these disagreements, once sources of friction, became opportunities for deeper understanding, for strengthening our collaborative bond.

We continued to discuss our plans for a family, our vision of a life lived with intention, purpose, and a profound sense of shared responsibility. The fear that had previously clouded our conversations had dissipated, replaced by a shared sense of excitement, a joyful anticipation of the challenges and rewards of parenthood.

The cottage in the countryside, once a distant dream, became a tangible goal. We started saving diligently, discussing paint colors, planning the layout of the garden. We even began experimenting with different recipes for homemade jam, a surprisingly therapeutic activity that underscored our shared commitment to building a life together.

The experience had not only strengthened our bond but also profoundly altered our relationship. We learned to appreciate the importance of vulnerability, of acknowledging our imperfections and weaknesses, of supporting each other

during times of adversity. We discovered the resilience of our partnership, the strength of our love, the depth of our shared commitment.

Our "taming" process, once viewed as a playful game of power dynamics, transformed into a journey of mutual respect, of understanding, of shared growth. We didn't conquer each other; we conquered our individual challenges, emerging stronger, wiser, and more deeply connected. The spice rack, once a battleground, now stood as a symbol of our shared culinary adventures, a testament to our resilience, a representation of the harmonious blend of our individual strengths.

This wasn't the ending of a fairy tale; it was the beginning of a new chapter, a chapter filled with the challenges and rewards of a life lived with purpose, with intention, with a profound sense of love, understanding, and a shared commitment to a future we would build, side-by-side, step by step, laugh by laugh. The laughter, the arguments, the quiet moments of shared contentment – all were integral parts of the tapestry of our evolving partnership, a tapestry woven with the threads of love, resilience, and an unshakeable commitment to navigating life's complexities together. The journey was far from over; the adventure, we both knew, had only just begun.

ADAPTING TO CHANGE

The countryside cottage, once a whimsical dream conjured during latenight discussions fueled by copious amounts of wine and increasingly ambitious plans, was now a tangible reality. The scent of freshly painted wood still hung in the air, a faint, sweet aroma mingling with the earthy perfume of the burgeoning spring garden. We'd chosen a muted sage green for the exterior, a color that Benedict, surprisingly, had insisted upon, declaring it "utterly sophisticated" with a wink that spoke volumes about the man he had become. Inside, the walls were a warm, creamy white, a blank canvas onto which we'd slowly begun to paint our shared story. Each piece of furniture, each carefully chosen artwork, whispered tales of our evolving relationship, a testament to our shared journey, our collective growth.

The transition hadn't been without its moments of friction. Moving from the bustling city to the serene tranquility of the countryside was a seismic shift, one that demanded flexibility and adaptability. Benedict, initially overwhelmed by the sudden change of pace, found himself grappling with a newfound sense of displacement. The structured routine of his corporate life, with its predictable rhythm and clearly defined goals, had been replaced by the open-ended expanse of rural existence, a landscape filled with unfamiliar challenges and unexpected opportunities.

"It's rather...quiet," he'd confessed one evening, staring out at the starstudded expanse of the night sky, his voice a low murmur against the backdrop of the chirping crickets. "Too quiet."

I smiled, understanding the undercurrent of his unease. The silence, once a source of peace and tranquility, now seemed to amplify his anxieties, the absence of the city's constant hum of activity highlighting his newfound idleness. His sudden redundancy had stripped him not only of his professional identity but also of a structured framework that had defined his daily life for so long.

It was a challenge we faced together, navigating the subtle currents of his adjustment with patience, understanding, and a healthy dose of humour. We discovered that adapting to change wasn't just about finding a new equilibrium; it was about reinventing ourselves, about rediscovering our individual strengths and weaknesses in the context of a new landscape. We became amateur gardeners, battling slugs and celebrating the emergence of vibrant sunflowers with equal enthusiasm. We learned to appreciate the quiet hum of contentment that permeated the countryside, a stark contrast to the frenetic energy of the city.

The evenings were filled with long conversations, sometimes punctuated by fits of laughter, sometimes by moments of quiet contemplation. We explored new culinary horizons, experimenting with recipes from old cookbooks, transforming our kitchen into a laboratory of gastronomical adventure. We rediscovered the pleasure of simple things: long walks in the woods, the thrill of finding the perfect mushroom, the satisfaction of a home-cooked meal shared in the glow of candlelight.

My "taming" project, once a playful game of witty banter and carefully orchestrated manipulations, had evolved into something far more profound. It wasn't about changing Benedict; it was about growing alongside him, supporting his evolution, celebrating his resilience. The spice rack, once a symbol of our playful power struggle, now represented a

harmonious blend of flavours, a metaphorical representation of our evolving relationship.

The screenplay we were collaborating on progressed slowly, hampered by the intermittent distractions of rural life, but it also blossomed in unexpected ways. The quiet solitude of the countryside allowed us to tap into a deeper well of creativity, freeing us from the relentless pressures of deadlines and expectations. Our creative differences, once sources of friction, became opportunities for deeper understanding, leading to more vibrant and insightful storytelling. We debated, we argued, we compromised, but the process strengthened our bond, forging a deeper connection through our shared passion.

There were moments of doubt, naturally. The financial adjustments to a simpler life required discipline and a shared commitment to managing our resources efficiently. The initial excitement of the move occasionally gave way to the monotony of rural routine, testing the limits of our patience and challenging the resilience of our relationship.

One rainy afternoon, huddled by the fire with mugs of steaming hot chocolate, Benedict confessed his anxieties about our future. "Do you ever wonder if we made a mistake?" he asked, his voice barely a whisper. "Leaving the city, changing everything...it feels like a gamble, doesn't it?"

I took his hand, my touch reassuring, my gaze unwavering. "Life is a series of gambles, my dear Benedict," I replied, my voice laced with both warmth and a hint of my signature sarcasm. "Some pay off handsomely, others teach us valuable lessons. This gamble, however, is one I'm willing to take again and again, because the prize is you, and the lessons are worth their weight in gold."

His response was a tender smile, a look that spoke of shared understanding and an unshakeable commitment to navigating life's complexities together. The gamble, indeed, was worth it. The cottage wasn't just a building; it was a sanctuary, a testament to our resilience, a symbol of our evolving relationship, a space where we could nurture our love, our dreams, and our shared journey towards a future that was still unfolding, one day, one laugh, one shared adventure at a time.

The arrival of our first child, a boisterous and undeniably charming little girl, was another significant catalyst for change, a transformative experience that redefined our priorities and reshaped our relationship yet again. The sleep- deprived nights, the endless diaper changes, the incessant demands of a tiny human – these challenges, initially daunting, became a source of profound bonding. We learned to navigate the complexities of parenthood together, sharing the responsibilities, supporting each other during moments of exhaustion and celebrating the small victories with shared joy.

Our shared creative projects took a backseat, of course, but this wasn't a retreat; it was a redirection of our energies, a re- evaluation of our priorities. The screenplay remained unfinished, a testament to the unpredictable nature of life and the ever-shifting priorities of parenthood. But the experience hadn't diminished our creative spirits; it had simply channeled them into new directions. We discovered a new form of storytelling, one that unfolded in the hushed tones of bedtime stories, in the impromptu songs we sang to our daughter, in the shared moments of laughter and connection that permeated our daily lives.

The cottage, once a symbol of our shared aspirations, now transformed into a haven, a place where we could nurture not just our relationship, but also the life of our growing family. The gardens, previously a source of shared amusement and occasional frustration, became a magical wonderland, filled with the wonder of wildflowers and the sweet scent of blossoming honeysuckle. The kitchen, once a laboratory of culinary experiments, now buzzed with the energy of family meals, the clinking of forks and spoons accompanying the laughter and chatter of a happy family.

Adapting to change wasn't a passive process; it was a dynamic journey, one that required flexibility, compromise, and a willingness to embrace the unexpected. Our relationship, once viewed through the lens of playful power dynamics, had evolved into something far deeper, far more profound. The "taming" process, if it could even be called that anymore, had transformed into a shared journey of self- discovery, a testament to our individual growth and the unwavering strength of our bond. We had learned to navigate the challenges, celebrate the successes, and cherish the moments of shared joy that punctuated our evolving lives, creating a tapestry woven with the vibrant threads of love, laughter, and unwavering commitment to a future that we were still actively creating, together. The adventure, as always, was only just beginning.

EMBRACING
THE FUTURE

The arrival of our daughter, Elsie, was less a gentle breeze and more a Category 5 hurricane of adorable chaos. Sleep became a mythical creature, whispered about in hushed tones during those rare moments of semi-consciousness. The pristine cottage, once a symbol of our carefully curated aesthetic, rapidly transformed into a charmingly chaotic landscape of spilled milk, misplaced toys, and a general air of delightful disarray. My meticulously planned spice rack, once a battlefield in our playful power struggle, was now frequently raided by tiny hands in search of something vaguely resembling a teething biscuit. Benedict, the once impeccably groomed city slicker, now sported perpetually sleep-deprived eyes and a charmingly dishevelled appearance that, I have to admit, had its own peculiar appeal.

The screenplay, long since abandoned, felt like a relic from a previous life, a whisper from a time when our world revolved around deadlines and creative differences rather than diaper changes and midnight feedings. Yet, oddly, the creative wellspring didn't dry up; it simply shifted its focus. Bedtime stories became impromptu improvisational theatre, our daughter's delighted squeals our only applause. The lullabies I sang, initially tentative and hesitant, evolved into confident, slightly off-key performances filled with invented verses and nonsensical rhymes. Benedict, surprisingly, possessed a hidden talent for creating elaborate, if slightly ludicrous, shadow puppets on the nursery wall, transforming ordinary objects into fantastical creatures that captivated our daughter's imagination.

Our conversations, once punctuated by witty barbs and intellectual sparring, now revolved around the minutiae of

childcare, the intricacies of baby sleep cycles, and the existential dread of weaning. Yet, paradoxically, amidst the whirlwind of parental responsibilities, our bond deepened. The shared exhaustion, the moments of quiet joy, the sheer overwhelming love for our tiny human – these experiences forged a connection that transcended the playful skirmishes of our earlier relationship. The "taming" process, if it could even be considered such anymore, had transformed into something much grander, a shared journey into the uncharted territory of parenthood, a collaborative adventure that tested our limits and strengthened our love in unexpected ways.

Financial constraints, once a source of mild anxiety, became a creative challenge. We adopted a more frugal lifestyle, embracing the simple pleasures of homegrown vegetables and homemade meals. Benedict, surprisingly adept at DIY projects, transformed discarded wood into whimsical toys, his craftsmanship far exceeding my initial expectations. The cottage, once a sanctuary of quiet contemplation, now pulsated with a frenetic, chaotic energy that was oddly exhilarating. It wasn't just a house; it was a testament to our adaptability, a reflection of our growing family, a vibrant hub where love, laughter, and a healthy dose of controlled chaos reigned supreme.

One evening, as we sat huddled on the sofa amidst a pile of toys, Elsie asleep in Benedict's arms, I looked at him, truly looked at him, and saw not the man I had initially sought to "tame," but a partner, a confidante, a loving father, and a true equal. The journey hadn't been easy; there were moments of doubt, moments of exhaustion, moments where the sheer weight of responsibility threatened to overwhelm us. But through it all, our love had endured, growing stronger, deeper, more resilient.

The future, once a vaguely defined horizon, now shimmered with possibilities. Elsie's laughter filled our days with joy, her tiny hand reaching for ours, a tangible reminder of the love that bound us. We had learned to navigate the unpredictable currents of life together, to embrace the unexpected twists and turns with grace and resilience.

There were moments of introspection, of course. Would we ever finish the screenplay? Would we ever rediscover that carefree, pre-parental existence? The answer, I realised, was less important than the journey itself. The "taming" was over, the game had changed. We weren't aiming for control, but for a shared understanding, a mutual respect that ran deeper than witty banter and meticulously planned spice racks.

The cottage, the garden, even the slightly chaotic nursery, had all become symbols not of control, but of shared growth, of evolving love, and of an unwavering commitment to the adventure ahead. The future, though uncertain, was filled with the promise of new beginnings, of new challenges, and, most importantly, of new shared experiences that would continue to shape and deepen our love. The journey wasn't about "taming" anymore; it was about the beautiful, messy, unpredictable journey of creating a life together, one filled with laughter, love, and the occasional, unavoidable, but ultimately endearing, chaos of parenthood. The true adventure, it seemed, was only just beginning.

The unexpected arrival of a second child, a

rambunctious little boy named Arthur, further solidified our evolution. Sleep deprivation became a way of life, a badge of honor worn with a weary but loving smile. The once tidy cottage embraced a new level of organised chaos. Toys multiplied exponentially, clothes lay scattered like fallen leaves, and the constant hum of activity became the new soundtrack of our days. Yet, amidst this delightful madness, a profound sense of completeness emerged. Our family, once a duo navigating the complexities of a new life in the countryside, had blossomed into a boisterous quartet, our love a sturdy ship navigating the stormy seas of parenthood with unwavering resolve.

Our creative pursuits remained largely dormant, overshadowed by the demands of caring for two young children. Yet, the creative spirit hadn't vanished; it simply adapted, finding expression in impromptu games, silly songs, and the creation of elaborate stories built around our children's ever-expanding imaginations. Our conversations, once peppered with witty banter and intellectual discourse, now revolved around the nuances of toddler tantrums, the intricacies of potty training, and the eternal quest for a moment's peace and quiet. But even within these mundane topics, a deeper connection emerged, a bond forged in the shared experiences of parenthood, a testament to our evolving relationship.

Financially, things remained tight. But the shared struggle, the collective effort to make ends meet, only served to strengthen our bond. We discovered a newfound appreciation for simple pleasures, for the warmth of a family meal, for the joy of a shared laugh amidst the chaos of daily life. The cottage, no longer a symbol of a carefully curated aesthetic, had transformed into a haven, a sanctuary where love, laughter, and family reigned supreme.

The "taming" of Benedict, a concept that once provided the narrative thread of our relationship, had long since faded.

The witty banter, the power plays, the subtly orchestrated manipulations – all of these had given way to something much more profound: a deep and abiding love, a partnership built on mutual respect, shared responsibilities, and an

unwavering commitment to our evolving family. The future remained uncertain, as it always does, but it was a future we faced together, our hands intertwined, our hearts united, our love a steadfast beacon guiding us through the ever-shifting landscape of life. And in that, we found a joy and contentment that transcended all else. The cottage, the children, the evolving partnership—it was all a testament to our shared journey, a reflection of a love that had grown stronger, deeper, and infinitely more profound than anything I could have ever imagined.

And that, my dear reader, is a story worth telling, again and again.

REFLECTION ON THE PAST

Looking back, the initial concept of "taming" Benedict seems almost laughably naive. It was a game, a playful rebellion against the tired tropes of romantic comedies, a witty exercise in subverting expectations. I envisioned myself as some sort of modern-day Katherine, a woman who wouldn't be subdued, a woman who would bend her man to her will, not through brute force, of course, but through the subtle art of manipulation, the strategic deployment of sarcasm, and a carefully curated collection of passive- aggressive gestures. I pictured a meticulously orchestrated campaign, a slow burn of witty barbs and pointed observations, each interaction a carefully calculated step towards my desired outcome.

The reality, of course, was far messier, far more unpredictable, and infinitely more rewarding. My initial strategy, a carefully constructed edifice of ironic detachment and calculated charm, crumbled almost immediately under the weight of actual, real-life connection.

Benedict, despite his initial displays of mild-mannered predictability, possessed an unexpected resilience, a surprising capacity for self-awareness, and a rather endearing tendency to turn my carefully laid plans into opportunities for genuine connection. My attempts to shape him into some idealized version of a partner, a carefully molded clay figure conforming to my preconceived notions, were met with unexpected resistance, not through outright defiance, but through a gentle, persistent refusal to be categorized.

He challenged my assumptions, questioned my motives, and often, to my utter frustration, managed to disarm me with a simple, genuine smile. The power plays I had envisioned, the

witty barbs intended to subtly nudge him towards my preferred behaviours, often resulted in uproarious laughter and unexpected moments of intimacy. He met my carefully crafted sarcasm with equally well-aimed wit, creating a dynamic dance of intellectual sparring that somehow, miraculously, strengthened rather than weakened our connection. The "taming" process, I realized with a touch of rueful amusement, was a two-way street. He was taming me, too.

He subtly challenged my fiercely independent nature, not through coercion or control, but through acts of kindness, through unexpected displays of vulnerability, and through a persistent, patient belief in my capacity for love. He saw beneath the carefully constructed façade of sarcastic indifference, recognizing the insecurity and the yearning for connection that lay hidden beneath. He didn't try to change me, he didn't try to force me into a mold, he simply accepted me, flaws and all. He embraced my eccentricities, celebrated my triumphs, and offered comforting support during my inevitable failures. And in that acceptance, in that unwavering belief in my authentic self, I found a freedom and a fulfillment that far exceeded anything my initial plans had anticipated.

The spice rack, once a battleground for playful power struggles, became a symbol of our shared culinary adventures. He learned to appreciate the nuances of my carefully curated collection of spices, marveling at the unexpected flavor combinations and complex aromas that transformed ordinary ingredients into culinary masterpieces. I, in turn, discovered a newfound appreciation for his simple, unpretentious approach to cooking, his inherent ability to transform basic ingredients into comforting, wholesome meals. The kitchen, once a theater for subtle manipulations, became a sanctuary of shared creativity and mutual support.

Our conversations, once punctuated by witty barbs and intellectual sparring, transformed into intimate dialogues, a shared exploration of our dreams, our fears, and our vulnerabilities. He listened, truly listened, offering thoughtful insights and unwavering support. I, in turn, found myself opening up, revealing aspects of myself I had previously kept hidden, shielded by the armor of sarcasm and ironic detachment. The transformation wasn't sudden; it was a gradual unfolding, a slow blossoming of trust and intimacy that deepened with each shared experience.

The arrival of Elsie, far from disrupting our carefully constructed equilibrium, reinforced the foundations of our evolving relationship. The shared exhaustion, the sleepless nights, the overwhelming joy of parenthood—these experiences forged a bond that transcended witty repartee and carefully orchestrated power plays. The "taming" was over, not because we had succeeded or failed in our individual goals, but because something far grander had emerged.

We were no longer engaging in a playful power struggle, but in a shared adventure, a collaborative journey into the often chaotic but ultimately rewarding world of parenthood. The cottage, once a stage for our carefully constructed charade, transformed into a haven of love, laughter, and the inevitable disarray of family life. Our individual identities remained intact, yet our connection deepened, our love expanding to encompass not just the two of us, but the tiny human who had so unexpectedly transformed our lives. The "taming," in the end, had given way to something far more significant: a love built on respect, on shared responsibility, and on a deep and unwavering commitment to building a life together.

And then came Arthur, the whirlwind of a younger brother who added a whole new level of chaos to our already vibrant household. He amplified the energy, the laughter, and the demands of parenthood. But he also, in his own rambunctious way, deepened our bonds. The shared responsibility of caring for two children intensified our teamwork, honed our patience, and solidified our commitment to each other. The "taming" narrative, once central to our story, faded into the background, replaced by a more profound narrative of partnership, shared purpose, and the ever-evolving dance of love, family, and life's unexpected surprises.

It wasn't a fairy tale ending, neatly tied up with a ribbon of perfect resolution. It was, instead, a messy, chaotic, incredibly rewarding reality. A reality filled with spilled milk, sleepless nights, and the sheer overwhelming joy of watching our children grow. A reality where the "taming" narrative had yielded to something far more substantial, far more meaningful, and far more fulfilling: the quiet strength of a love that had grown, evolved, and ultimately redefined the meaning of partnership. The spice rack remained, a symbol not of control, but of shared culinary adventures. The cottage, once a stage for a carefully orchestrated game, had become a testament to the beautiful, unpredictable journey of family life. And in that journey, in that messy, beautiful reality, we found something far more profound than the playful power struggles of our initial encounters. We found something real, something enduring, something truly transformative. We found love. And that, it turned out, was the greatest adventure of all.

THE MEANING
OF TAMING

So, the "taming" – that initial, almost childish game of wills – what was it, really? Looking back, it seems less a conquest and more a clumsy, albeit entertaining, stumble towards something far deeper. My carefully crafted strategy, born from a desire to subvert expectations and rewrite the tired narrative of the "shrew" and her "taming," was, in hindsight, laughably inadequate. I had envisioned a calculated chess match, a battle of wits where I, the modern-day Katherine, would emerge victorious, having molded Benedict into a perfectly sculpted partner, reflecting my own desires and expectations.

The irony, of course, is that I underestimated Benedict, his subtle resilience, and the unexpected power of genuine connection. My sarcastic barbs, intended as carefully placed landmines, often detonated into fits of laughter, revealing a shared sense of humor that transcended our initial power play. His quiet strength challenged my assumptions about control and dominance, subtly forcing me to reconsider my own deeply ingrained beliefs about relationships and power dynamics. He didn't resist my attempts at "taming" through overt defiance; instead, he engaged, challenged, and ultimately, disarmed me with his gentle persistence, his vulnerability, and his unwavering belief in the possibility of something real between us.

He saw beyond the carefully constructed walls of my sarcastic exterior, recognizing the yearning for intimacy, the fear of vulnerability, that lay hidden beneath. He accepted my quirks, my eccentricities, my sometimes overwhelming need for independence. He didn't attempt to "fix" me, to reshape me into a more palatable version of myself; he loved me, flaws and all. And in that acceptance, in that unwavering belief in my authenticity, I found a freedom I hadn't known was possible. The "taming" became a mutual process, a reciprocal shaping of identities, not a conquest, but a collaboration.

The spice rack, that battlefield of my initial power plays, ironically became a symbol of our evolving connection. Initially, the spices themselves were tools – carefully selected to either tantalize or repel, depending on Benedict's culinary choices, and whether he aligned with my superior taste. Now, it stands as a testament to shared culinary adventures, to the joy of discovering new flavors together, to the unexpected harmony found in our vastly different approaches to cooking.

Our conversations, once a playground of witty repartee and intellectual sparring, deepened into intimate dialogues, explorations of vulnerability and shared fears. We no longer used words to test each other, but to reveal ourselves. The barriers I had constructed around my heart crumbled, brick by brick, under the weight of his genuine kindness and unwavering support. He listened, truly listened, not just to my words, but to the unspoken anxieties and desires that lay beneath. I, in turn, found the courage to be truly open, to shed the armor of sarcasm, and to embrace the vulnerability that comes with authentic connection.

The arrival of Elsie, our daughter, further reshaped our understanding of "taming." The exhaustion, the sleepless nights, the overwhelming joy – these shared experiences forged a bond that went beyond witty exchanges and calculated power plays. It was a bond forged in the crucible of shared responsibility, a shared commitment to nurturing a new life. The "taming" narrative, once our primary story, faded into the background, overshadowed by a far more

profound narrative: the building of a family, a shared journey into parenthood.

And then came Arthur, our son, a whirlwind of energy and chaos. He was, in essence, the ultimate test of our newly defined relationship. He amplified everything – the exhaustion, the laughter, the sheer, overwhelming demands of parenthood. But he also intensified our love, our patience, and our mutual support. The shared responsibility of caring for two children not only strengthened our teamwork, but honed our individual capabilities. We learned to adapt, to improvise, to rely on each other implicitly. The old "taming" script simply couldn't contain the complexity, the chaos, the overwhelming joy of our family life.

Our "taming" narrative, once the driving force of our relationship, transformed into a story of partnership, of shared purpose, of evolving intimacy. It wasn't a fairytale ending, with perfectly resolved conflicts and neatly tied bows. It was messy, unpredictable, chaotic, and ultimately, deeply fulfilling. It was a story of learning, of growth, of mutual respect, and of a love that had defied my initial, somewhat arrogant plans for control.

The spice rack remains, a testament not to control, but to the shared joys of culinary creativity. The cottage, once the stage for our carefully constructed game, became a haven, a sanctuary of love and laughter, amidst the inevitable disarray of family life. The old definition of "taming," that image of domination and control, is a thing of the past. It has been replaced by something far more meaningful, far more enduring: the quiet strength of a love built on mutual respect, on shared responsibility, on a deep and unwavering commitment to building a life together. And in that journey, in that beautiful, messy reality, we discovered the true meaning of love, a love that transcends games, outmaneuvering any carefully constructed plans for control. We found something real, enduring, and transformative. We found love, and that, I discovered, was the greatest adventure of all. It wasn't about taming each other, but about taming our own preconceived notions of love, partnership, and the power dynamics within a relationship. And in that, perhaps, lay the true, unexpected victory.

The lessons learned went far beyond the initial playful power struggle. They extended to my understanding of myself, of my own needs, and my own capacity for vulnerability. I had entered the relationship with a preconceived notion of what a relationship should be, a clear vision of how to mold a partner to my preferences. The reality, however, proved far more complex, forcing me to shed the armor of sarcasm and embrace a deeper level of intimacy and connection. I learned that true intimacy isn't about control, but about acceptance.

It's not about bending someone to your will, but about growing together, supporting each other, and celebrating each other's unique strengths and flaws. The "taming" process, as it turned out, tamed me more than it did Benedict. It challenged my preconceived notions, shattered my carefully constructed walls, and forced me to confront my own insecurities and vulnerabilities.

And perhaps, that was the most valuable lesson of all. The process of "taming" wasn't about controlling another person, but about learning to control my own expectations, my own need to be in control. It was a journey of self-discovery, of recognizing my own limitations, and of embracing the unexpected joys and challenges of a love that defies easy categorization or control. It was a messy, chaotic, and ultimately beautiful journey, and the destination was something far more meaningful than I had ever imagined. It was a love that continues to evolve, to adapt, and to grow, a testament to the power of mutual respect, shared

responsibility, and the unwavering commitment to building a life together. The story of our "taming," therefore, is not a story of conquest, but a story of transformation, a story of growth, and a story of love. It's a story of acceptance, of understanding, and of the unexpected beauty found in embracing the messy, unpredictable reality of family life.

A LASTING PARTNERSHIP

The years that followed were a blur of milestones and memories, a tapestry woven with the threads of laughter, tears, and the quiet hum of domesticity. Elsie blossomed into a bright, inquisitive child, her laughter echoing through the cottage, a constant reminder of the boundless joy she brought into our lives. Arthur, ever the whirlwind, followed close behind, his boundless energy a testament to the enduring power of sibling rivalry and the unwavering love that underpinned it. The cottage, once the stage for our carefully orchestrated power plays, transformed into a vibrant, chaotic hub of family life, a testament to the unexpected harmony that had blossomed from our initial, somewhat contentious courtship.

The spice rack, once a symbol of our playful battle of wills, now stood as a monument to our shared culinary adventures. It wasn't just about meticulously chosen spices anymore; it was about experimenting with flavors, sharing recipes, and the occasional culinary disaster that only served to strengthen our bond. Benedict, once hesitant in the kitchen, had blossomed into a surprisingly competent chef, his culinary skills evolving alongside our relationship. He still couldn't quite match my precise approach to spicing, but his willingness to learn, to experiment, to embrace the occasional kitchen mishap, was a testament to his growth, his adaptability, and his unwavering support.

Our conversations, once sharp and witty exchanges, evolved into deeper, more meaningful dialogues. The sarcasm, once a weapon in our game of wills, softened into a shared language of affection, a subtle undercurrent in our everyday conversations. We discussed everything – from the mundane realities of grocery shopping to the deeper philosophical questions about life, death, and everything in between. The discussions were no longer about one-upmanship, but about mutual understanding, about exploring each other's thoughts and feelings without judgment.

We learned to navigate the complexities of parenthood together, our initial anxieties and disagreements slowly giving way to a seamless collaboration. The division of labor wasn't always equal, but it was always fair. We adapted to each other's strengths and weaknesses, filling the gaps, supporting each other through the inevitable exhaustion and the overwhelming joy of raising a family. The late-night feedings, the early morning diaper changes, the countless school runs – these weren't burdens, but shared experiences that strengthened our bond, forging a connection that went far beyond the initial playful power struggle.

The unexpected challenges – the illness, the school plays, the sibling squabbles – these weren't obstacles, but opportunities for growth, opportunities to demonstrate our unwavering commitment to each other, our children, and the family we had built together. We learned to communicate more effectively, to listen more attentively, to appreciate each other's contributions, even amidst the chaos of everyday life. Our love wasn't a constant state of blissful harmony; it was a dynamic force, capable of weathering storms, adapting to change, and emerging stronger from every challenge.

It wasn't about taming each other; it was about taming the expectations we had brought into the relationship. We had both entered with preconceived notions of what a relationship should be, of what a partner should be like. We had both expected a certain level of control, a certain amount of predictability. But life, as always, had other plans.

The unexpected twists and turns, the challenges and triumphs,

these were not disruptions to our carefully crafted plans; they were the very essence of our love story.

The years melted into a continuum of shared experiences, shaping us, molding us into something more than the sum of our individual parts. We weren't just a couple; we were a team, a family, a partnership built on mutual respect, shared responsibility, and a love that had defied all attempts to define or control it. The laughter, the tears, the quiet moments of shared intimacy – these were the building blocks of our lasting partnership.

The cottage, with its overflowing spice rack and the ever- present aroma of freshly baked bread, became a sanctuary, a haven of love and laughter. It was a place where our individual stories converged, where our separate identities merged, where two distinct individuals became something far greater, something more enduring, something more beautiful than either of us could have imagined.

The "taming" narrative, that initial game of wills, faded into the background, becoming a distant memory, a curious footnote in the larger, more significant story of our lives together. It was a reminder of where we had started, of the initial struggles, the misunderstandings, the playful battle of wills that had inadvertently paved the way for something far more profound and enduring.

Our relationship wasn't a fairy tale; it was a realistic portrayal of a love story, complete with its share of challenges, setbacks, and unexpected detours. It was a story of growth, of learning, of adaptation, of compromise. It was a story of two individuals, each with their own unique flaws and eccentricities, learning to navigate the complexities of life together, learning to embrace the unpredictable nature of love and family life.

And as we stood, years later, surrounded by the laughter and chaos of our family, I realized that the true "taming" hadn't been about controlling each other, but about controlling our own expectations, about accepting the messy, unpredictable, and ultimately beautiful reality of a life lived together. It was about taming our own egos, our own need to control, and embracing the unexpected joys of a life lived fully, authentically, and with unwavering love. That, I realized, was the greatest adventure of all – not a carefully orchestrated conquest, but a lifelong journey of mutual growth, shared responsibility, and enduring love. And in that messy, unpredictable, wonderfully imperfect journey, we discovered the true meaning of "taming," a meaning far richer and more enduring than any carefully crafted script could ever express. We found not control, but connection.

Not conquest, but companionship. Not dominance, but devotion. And in that, we found our happily ever after.

LOOKING TOWARDS THE HORIZON

The scent of woodsmoke and roasting chestnuts hung heavy in the crisp autumn air, a comforting aroma that mirrored the warmth settling deep within my heart. Benedict, his usual chaotic energy tempered by a quiet contentment, sat beside me, Elsie nestled between us, her small hand clutching a

half-eaten gingerbread man. Arthur, predictably, was causing a minor ruckus in the background, engaging in a spirited debate with a particularly stubborn squirrel over the merits of acorn versus hazelnut. The scene, chaotic yet perfectly harmonious, epitomized the life we had carefully, and sometimes haphazardly, built together.

It hadn't been a straightforward journey. The initial spark, that witty battle of wills, had been both exhilarating and exhausting. We'd clashed over everything from the optimal brewing temperature of Earl Grey to the philosophical implications of alphabetizing spice racks. But through it all, a deeper connection had been forged, a bond built not on control, but on a shared understanding of our respective quirks and a mutual appreciation for a good, well-placed sarcastic remark.

"Remember that disastrous attempt at soufflé?" Benedict chuckled, his eyes twinkling with amusement, a memory bringing a smile to my lips. "The kitchen looked like a scene from a culinary crime thriller."

I grinned, shaking my head. "And your insistence on using saffron in the shepherd's pie? A culinary abomination if ever there was one."

Elsie, ever perceptive, piped up, "Daddy's cooking is better now, Mummy."

Arthur, momentarily distracted from his squirrel negotiation, added, "Except for that time he tried to make pancakes from scratch. Those were... interesting."

The laughter that erupted was genuine, a testament to the easy camaraderie that had replaced the initial tension. We had learned to laugh at our mistakes, to appreciate the absurdities of everyday life, and to find joy in the chaos. The "taming" process, if it could even be called that, had transformed into something far more profound – a journey of mutual respect, shared growth, and a deep, abiding love.

Our lives weren't some perfectly crafted rom-com scenario. There were moments of frustration, disagreements over bedtime routines, and the occasional silent treatment (usually initiated by me, I admit). But these were merely minor blips on the radar of a life teeming with joy, laughter, and the profound satisfaction of building a family together. We had learned to navigate the complexities of adult relationships, accepting the imperfections, embracing the unpredictable, and celebrating the shared victories.

Looking back, the initial power struggle, the playful attempt to "tame" each other, now seemed almost quaint. It had served as a catalyst, a starting point, but the real magic had occurred in the quiet moments, in the shared laughter, in the subtle gestures of affection, in the unspoken understanding that had blossomed over time.

We had evolved. Benedict, once resistant to any form of domesticity, had become an enthusiastic participant in family life. He read bedtime stories, helped with homework, even mastered the art of braiding Elsie's hair (though Arthur

remains fiercely opposed to any form of hair-related intervention). His transformation hadn't been a result of coercion, but of his own willingness to embrace a life beyond his initial expectations. He had found his own definition of "home," a place where he felt loved, respected, and genuinely happy.

And I, too, had evolved. The fiercely independent woman who had initially embarked on this playful game of dominance had discovered the profound satisfaction of shared responsibility, of mutual support, and of building a life alongside someone who valued and respected her fiercely independent spirit. I had learned that true strength wasn't about controlling another person, but about finding strength in vulnerability, in collaboration, and in the unconditional love that bound us together.

The spice rack, once a battleground, now stood as a testament to our shared culinary adventures, a symbol of our evolving relationship. It wasn't just about alphabetization anymore; it was about experimenting with new flavors, trying out obscure recipes, and laughing over the occasional culinary disaster. The spices themselves were a metaphor – a blend of flavors, sometimes clashing, sometimes harmonizing, but always adding depth and complexity to the tapestry of our lives.

The future stretched before us, a canvas of possibilities painted with hues of hope, excitement, and a profound sense of contentment. We didn't have all the answers, and certainly not a perfectly crafted plan.

Life, as we had both learned, was far too unpredictable for that. But we had something far more valuable – a love that had weathered storms, a partnership built on mutual respect, and a family that filled our lives with joy, laughter, and the comforting aroma of roasting chestnuts and woodsmoke.

The "taming" narrative had served its purpose, a playful backdrop to a more profound story. It was a reminder of our journey, of the initial sparks, the playful battles, the gradual understanding, and the ultimate acceptance of our imperfections and our strengths. We had learned to appreciate the messy, chaotic, and wonderfully imperfect reality of life together, realizing that true love wasn't about control, but about connection, about companionship, and about the enduring power of mutual respect.

As the sun dipped below the horizon, casting long shadows across the garden, I held Benedict's hand, feeling the warmth of his touch, the comfort of his presence. Elsie, nestled snugly between us, was drifting off to sleep, her quiet breaths a gentle rhythm in the stillness of the evening.

Arthur, miraculously subdued, sat quietly watching the squirrels scamper up a tree. This was our "happily ever after," not a fairy-tale ending, but a testament to a life lived fully, authentically, and with an unwavering love that defied any simplistic definition. It was a love born not of taming, but of acceptance, understanding, and a shared commitment to the beautiful messiness of life together. And that, I realized, was far more satisfying than any carefully crafted script could ever hope to express. It was the quiet, enduring joy of a life lived well, a love story still unfolding, chapter by chapter, with each day a new adventure, a new opportunity to deepen the connection, to nurture the bond, and to celebrate the simple, profound beauty of our shared existence. The horizon beckoned, promising more adventures, more challenges, and more opportunities to discover the ever-evolving definition of our love, a love that continually redefined itself, growing stronger, more profound, and more beautiful with each passing year. The spice rack, a quiet witness to our journey, held the promise of countless more culinary adventures, mirroring the infinite

possibilities that lay ahead, a testament to our ongoing, ever- evolving, and uniquely beautiful story.

A LASTING IMPRESSION

The crisp autumn air, still carrying the scent of woodsmoke and roasted chestnuts, held a different kind of magic now, a quiet stillness that spoke of contentment and the gentle hum of settled lives. Benedict, his hand resting lightly on Elsie's back as she toddled ahead, looked remarkably less like the whirlwind of chaotic energy he'd once been and more like a man utterly at peace. Even Arthur, usually a tempest of furry frustration, seemed strangely subdued, content to trail behind, occasionally pausing to sniff a particularly intriguing blade of grass. The image, etched in the golden light of the late afternoon, was a perfect postcard of domestic bliss, a stark contrast to the initial tempestuous meeting of wills that had launched this unexpected journey.

Looking back, the "taming" had been less a process of subjugation and more a series of exquisitely orchestrated compromises. It wasn't about bending one another to a pre-conceived ideal, but about recognizing and celebrating the unique strengths and quirks that made us who we were. The initial sparks, the witty clashes over everything from the merits of a perfectly brewed Earl Grey to the existential dread of mismatched socks, now seemed like amusing anecdotes, charming relics of a time when we were still learning to navigate the unpredictable waters of our relationship.

Benedict, the man who once considered alphabetizing his spice rack an act of unspeakable tyranny, now not only alphabetized, but categorized by region, flavor profile, and even historical significance. He had become a culinary adventurer, his once-limited repertoire now encompassing everything from perfectly executed French pastries to surprisingly authentic Indian curries. His transformation hadn't been a forced march, but a delightful exploration of a life he hadn't envisioned, a life enriched by shared experiences and a growing appreciation for domesticity.

My own evolution had been equally profound. The fiercely independent woman who had embarked on this playful game of "taming," initially seeking to mold him to her image, had instead discovered the unexpected joy of shared responsibility and the unexpected beauty of collaborative living. The initial power dynamic, which had felt so important then, had been replaced by a quiet strength that arose from mutual respect and a deeply fulfilling partnership. I had learned that true strength wasn't about controlling another person but finding strength in vulnerability, in the shared weight of responsibility, in the quiet understanding that blooms between two people truly committed to each other's growth.

The children, of course, had been the unexpected catalyst, the glue that bound our initially disparate lives together.

Elsie, with her infectious laughter and boundless curiosity, had melted away years of ingrained societal expectations and replaced them with a shared commitment to nurturing a loving and supportive environment. Arthur, despite his ongoing aversion to hairbrushes, had provided a running commentary on our lives, a comedic counterpoint to our shared adventures, his relentless energy a testament to the sheer unpredictability of raising a small human who viewed squirrels as his intellectual equals.

There had been moments, of course, when the carefully constructed façade of domestic tranquility had threatened to crumble. Sleepless nights, screaming toddlers, and the occasional eruption over the seemingly insignificant – the eternal debate over the optimal temperature for the

dishwasher, for example – had tested the very foundations of our carefully constructed lives. But even in those moments, in the midst of the chaos and frustration, we had found our way back to each other, our shared commitment to each other serving as a steady anchor in the swirling currents of parenthood.

Our family, far from being a perfectly staged tableau, was a vibrant, chaotic tapestry, woven with threads of laughter, tears, triumphs, and the occasional spectacular failure. We didn't have all the answers, certainly not a perfectly crafted roadmap to a happy ever after. But we had something far more valuable: a genuine connection, a deep and abiding love that had grown stronger with each passing challenge. The "taming" narrative, initially a playful construct, had become a metaphor for our journey – a journey of self- discovery, mutual respect, and the realization that true happiness lies not in control, but in connection.

The spice rack, once a battlefield, now stood as a testament to our shared culinary adventures, a silent witness to our evolving relationship. It was no longer just about alphabetization; it was about the discovery of new flavors, the thrill of experimenting with unexpected combinations, and the shared laughter that inevitably followed any culinary mishaps. Each spice, with its unique aroma and flavor profile, represented a facet of our evolving relationship – sometimes clashing, sometimes complementing, always adding depth and complexity to the rich tapestry of our shared lives. The spices themselves were a symbol, a reminder of the messy, unpredictable, and ultimately beautiful journey of life together.

As the sun dipped below the horizon, painting the sky in hues of fiery orange and soft lavender, I looked at Benedict, his face softened by the gentle light, his eyes reflecting the

warmth of our shared life. Elsie, nestled in his arms, was fast asleep, her peaceful breathing a gentle lullaby against the evening stillness. Arthur, unusually quiet, was content to observe the world from his perch on Benedict's lap. This was our "happily ever after," not a fairytale ending, but a testament to the simple, profound beauty of a life lived authentically, a life built on mutual respect, unwavering love, and the shared commitment to navigating the messy, unpredictable, and wonderfully imperfect reality of family life.

This wasn't a story about taming, but about growth. About accepting imperfections, embracing the unexpected, and celebrating the quiet victories along the way. It was about discovering that true strength lies not in control, but in vulnerability, in shared responsibility, and in the enduring power of a love that transcends any simplistic definition. It was the story of two people, initially locked in a playful battle of wills, who found their way to a love that was as unpredictable, as chaotic, and

as beautiful as life itself. A love that continually redefined itself, deepening, evolving, and becoming more profound with each passing year. A love that had found its own unique, beautiful definition, far beyond the simple notion of "taming." It was a love story still unfolding, chapter by chapter, a testament to the enduring power of connection, a promise of future adventures, and a quiet confidence that our messy, beautiful life together would continue to unfold in its own wonderfully unpredictable way, a tapestry woven with the threads of laughter, love, and the lingering scent of woodsmoke and roasted chestnuts on a crisp autumn evening. And that, I realized, was far more satisfying than any carefully crafted script could ever hope to express.

ACKNOWLEDGMENTS

First and foremost, a massive thank you to my agent, who somehow managed to keep her sanity while dealing with my endless stream of sarcastic emails and questionable plot bunnies. To my editor, your insightful feedback and unwavering belief in this project (despite my frequent attempts to sabotage it with badly-written puns) are deeply appreciated. A special shout-out to my beta readers, whose brutal honesty and surprisingly hilarious comments saved me from a number of potential literary catastrophes. And finally, to my long-suffering partner, who endured countless nights of me muttering about

Shakespeare, you're a saint. (Although, you still haven't alphabetized the spice rack...)

APPENDIX

This appendix contains, for the truly dedicated reader (or masochist), a comparative analysis of Shakespeare's *The Taming of the Shrew* and my hilariously superior reimagining. Spoiler alert: I win.

PHILOSOPHICAL COMPARATIVE ANALYSIS OF SHAKESPEARE'S "THE TAMING OF THE SHREW"

BY KATHERINE

INTRODUCTION

William Shakespeare's "The Taming of the Shrew" has long

been a source of fascination for scholars, critics, and audiences alike. The play's intricate dynamics between gender, power, and identity offer fertile ground for philosophical inquiry. As the main character, Katherine, I have found myself at the heart of these discussions, embodying the complex interplay of autonomy and submission. This paper aims to explore the philosophical dimensions of "The Taming of the Shrew," examining the themes of freedom, identity, and interpersonal relationships through a comparative lens.

FREEDOM AND AUTONOMY

The concept of freedom is central to any philosophical discussion of "The Taming of the Shrew." Katherine's journey can be seen as a struggle for autonomy within a patriarchal society that seeks to suppress her individuality. The play's depiction of marriage and the societal expectations placed upon women bring to light the tension between personal freedom and social conformity. Through a comparative analysis, we can explore how other philosophical works address the balance between individual autonomy and societal norms.

STOICISM AND ACCEPTANCE

Stoicism, the ancient philosophy that advocates for accepting the things we cannot change while focusing on our internal virtues, offers one perspective on Katherine's transformation.

Stoic thinkers such as Epictetus and Marcus Aurelius emphasize the importance of inner freedom, suggesting that true autonomy comes from within. Katherine's eventual acceptance of her role in society can be interpreted through the lens of Stoicism, as she learns to navigate her external circumstances while preserving her inner dignity.

EXISTENTIALISM AND AUTHENTICITY

Existentialist philosophers like Jean-Paul Sartre and Simone de Beauvoir challenge the notion of predetermined roles, advocating for authentic self-expression and the rejection of societal constraints. Katherine's initial resistance to her prescribed role as a submissive wife aligns with existentialist ideals of authenticity and rebellion against conformity. By comparing Katherine's journey with existentialist principles, we can gain insights into the struggle for self-definition and the quest for genuine freedom.

IDENTITY AND SELF-PERCEPTION

Identity is another key theme in "The Taming of the Shrew," with Katherine's evolving selfperception serving as a focal point. The play's exploration of identity raises questions about the nature of selfhood and the influence of external forces on our sense of self.

SOCIAL CONSTRUCTIVISM AND ROLE-PLAYING

Social constructivist theories, such as those proposed by George Herbert Mead and Erving Goffman, suggest that identity is shaped by social interactions and the roles we play in society. Katherine's identity shifts as she navigates her relationships with Petruchio and others, reflecting the fluidity of self-perception in response to social expectations. By examining Katherine's experience through the lens of social constructivism, we can better understand the dynamic nature of identity formation.

PSYCHOANALYTIC PERSPECTIVES

Psychoanalytic theorists like Sigmund Freud and Carl Jung offer another perspective on identity, emphasizing the role of the unconscious mind and internal conflicts in shaping selfperception. Katherine's interactions with Petruchio can be seen as a manifestation of deeper psychological struggles, as she grapples with her desires for autonomy and acceptance. By analyzing Katherine's journey through psychoanalytic principles, we can uncover the subconscious influences on her evolving identity.

INTERPERSONAL RELATIONSHIPS AND POWER DYNAMICS

The relationships between characters in "The Taming of the Shrew" highlight the complexities of power dynamics and interpersonal connections. Katherine's interactions with Petruchio, her father, and other characters reveal the intricate balance of power and influence within social relationships.

FEMINIST CRITIQUES

Feminist philosophers like Judith Butler and bell hooks provide critical insights into the gendered power dynamics at play in "The Taming of the Shrew." Katherine's struggle against patriarchal control and her eventual submission can be examined through feminist critiques of power, autonomy, and the societal expectations imposed upon women. By comparing Katherine's experience with feminist theories, we can explore the broader implications of gender roles and power structures.

RELATIONAL ETHICS

Relational ethics, as proposed by philosophers like Carol Gilligan and Nel Noddings, emphasize the importance of empathy, care, and mutual respect in interpersonal relationships. Katherine's journey can be seen as a quest for relational harmony, as she navigates the complexities of her relationships with Petruchio and others. By examining Katherine's experience through the lens of relational ethics, we can gain insights into the role of empathy and care in fostering genuine connections.

CONCLUSION

"The Taming of the Shrew" offers a rich tapestry of philosophical themes that continue to resonate with audiences and scholars. Katherine's journey of self-discovery, autonomy, and relational dynamics provides a compelling case study for exploring the intersections of freedom, identity, and interpersonal relationships. By examining the play through various philosophical lenses, we can uncover deeper insights into the human experience and the enduring quest for authenticity and connection.

REFERENCES

- Shakespeare, William. The Taming of the Shrew. (Because even I can't completely ignore the source material.)
- Brunvand, J. H. (1991). The taming of the shrew (Routledge revivals): A comparative study of oral and literary versions (1st ed.). Routledge.
- Book Review University. (n.d.). The comparative analysis of The Taming of the Shrew by William Shakespeare and Lysistrata by Aristophanes. Retrieved from [URL]
- Various online dictionaries and thesauruses, for those times when my vocabulary failed me.
- My therapist, for keeping me sane while writing.
- Numerous articles on the complexities of modern relationships (mainly to confirm my own cynical observations).

GLOSSARY

Benedict: A perfectly ordinary man, initially resistant to even the most basic concepts of organization, eventually charmed into domestic bliss (and alphabetizing his spice rack).

Katherine: A fiercely independent woman, not remotely interested in being "tamed," only in finding someone with a sufficiently high tolerance for witty banter.

Earl Grey: A superior tea, a frequent source of contention in the early stages of Benedict's domestication. (He eventually learned to appreciate it.)

Arthur: A fluffy terror of a dog whose opinions on life are often overlooked but nevertheless profoundly insightful.

Elsie: A small human, capable of immense destruction and even more immense cuteness.

REFERENCES

Shakespeare, William. *The Taming of the Shrew* . (Because even I can't completely ignore the source material.) Various online dictionaries and thesauruses, for those times when my vocabulary failed me. My therapist, for keeping me sane while writing. Numerous articles on the complexities of modern relationships (mainly to confirm my own cynical observations).

- Shakespeare, W. (2016). *The taming of the shrew*. In S. Greenblatt, W. Cohen, J. E.

  Howard, & K. Eisaman Maus (Eds.), *The Norton Shakespeare: Essential plays, sonnets* (3rd ed., pp. 583-649). W.W. Norton & Company.

- Merriam-Webster. (n.d.). *Resilience.* In Merriam-Webster.com dictionary. Retrieved October 26, 2023, from https://www.merriam-webster.com/dictionary/resilience

- Oxford University Press. (n.d.). *Well-being.* In Oxford English Dictionary. Retrieved October 26, 2023, from https://www.oed.com/

- Thesaurus.com. (n.d.). *Harmony.* In Thesaurus.com. Retrieved October 26, 2023, from https://www.thesaurus.com/browse/harmony

- Brown, L. (2023). Navigating Love in the Digital Age. *Cosmopolitan Magazine*. Retrieved from [URL4]
- Green, P. (2022). The Modern Relationship Dilemma. *Time Magazine*. Retrieved from [URL5]
- Johnson, S. (2021). The Changing Dynamics of Partnership. *Vogue*. Retrieved from [URL6]
- Smith, T. (2020). Love, Lust, and Technology: A Deep Dive. *Forbes*. Retrieved from [URL7]
- Adams, D. (2019). Balancing Career and Romance. *GQ Magazine*. Retrieved from [URL8]
- Williams, K. (2018). Communication Challenges in Modern Love. *The Atlantic*. Retrieved from [URL9]
- Lee, H. (2017). The Rise of Long-Distance Relationships. *Elle Magazine*. Retrieved from [URL10]
- Martinez, R. (2016). The Role of Social Media in Modern Romance. *New Yorker*. Retrieved from [URL11]
- Garcia, M. (2015). Understanding Commitment in the 21st Century. *Harper's Bazaar*. Retrieved from [URL12]
- Harris, J. (2014). The Effect of Pop Culture on Relationships. *Rolling Stone*. Retrieved from [URL13]

LISTING:

The URLs listed in the document are intended to provide additional references and sources for the information discussed.

1. **Merriam-Webster (Resilience)** - [URL: https://www.merriam-webster.com/dictionary/resilience - This URL is referenced in the "References" section.

2. **Oxford University Press (Well-being)** -[URL: https://www.oed.com/ - This URL is referenced in the "References" section.

3. **Thesaurus.com (Harmony)** - [URL: https://www.thesaurus.com/browse/harmony - This URL is referenced in the "References" section.

4. **Cosmopolitan Magazine (Navigating Love in the Digital Age)** - [URL: https://www.cosmopolitan.com/dating-inthe-digital-age/] - This URL fits in the context of the relationship dynamics and modern romance references.

5. **Time Magazine (The Modern Relationship Dilemma)** - [URL: https://time.com/5402188/how-to-fight-healthypartner/] - This would be relevant in discussions about modern relationship challenges.

6. **Vogue (The Changing Dynamics of Partnership)** - [URL: https://vogue.com/] - This URL provides context on changing dynamics in partnerships.

7. **Forbes (Love, Lust, and Technology: A Deep Dive)** - [URL: https://forbes.com/]

8. **GQ Magazine (Balancing Career and Romance)** - [URL: https://www.gq.com/] - This URL fits in the context of balancing professional and personal life.

9. **The Atlantic (Communication Challenges in Modern Love)** - [URL: https://www.theatlantic.com/] - This URL references communication issues in modern relationships.

10. **Elle Magazine (The Rise of Long-Distance Relationships)** - [URL: https://www.elle.com/uk/life-andculture/culture/a62839326/long-distance-friendship/] - This URL is relevant for discussions on long-distance relationships..com/

11. **New Yorker (The Role of Social Media in Modern Romance)** - [URL: https://newyorker.com/] This URL is relevant for the role of social media in modern romance.

12. **Harper's Bazaar (Understanding Commitment in the 21st Century)** - [URL: https://harpersbazaar.com/] - This reference is used for understanding commitment in modern times.

13.   **Rolling Stone (The Effect of Pop Culture on Relationships)** - [URL: https://www.rollingstone.com/] - This URL is relevant for discussing pop culture's impact on relationships.

AUTHOR BIOGRAPHY

Aurealia Nelson is a writer who believes that the best way to deal with the absurdity of modern life is through witty social commentary and a generous helping of bitter, blank sarcasm. She started a degree in British Literature (which she mostly uses to impress people at parties) and has ADHD with a secret passion for alphabetizing things. When not battling plot bunnies or trying to convince her cats that she is, in fact, the Supreme Ruler of the Universe, she can be found attempting (and often failing) to achieve a state of domestic tranquility. Her other works include _Sacred Ashes_, _It was the Cat_ (go figure), _Rubbed the Wrong Way_, and _Whispers from the 5th Dimension_, _The Velvet Cage_, and _Pear, Pear Over There_ (Children's Book) as well as other works that can be found on aurealianelson.com. She accepts applications for personal chefs and professional spice rack organizers.

www.ingramcontent.com/pod-product-compliance
Lightning Source LLC
Chambersburg PA
CBHW070629260626
47161CB00007B/2642